AN ISLAND
MYSTERY

By

Michael A Greaves

This book is dedicated to my wife Jan,
who encouraged me to try my hand at writing and fortunately
persisted in her cajoling until I did,
and also to my two sons, Andrew and Mathew,
both of whom I am immensely proud of.

CONTENTS

I would like to thank Alan and Doreen Carroll and Haydn Griffith, my good friends from back home in Lancashire, who were kind enough to read the first draft copy of *An Island Mystery* and provide me with very positive feedback.

I would also like to thank The Kinmel Arms in Moelfre for a lot of the inspiration for the storylines and the refreshment it provided during the writing of this book.

PART ONE

Chapter 1

The man who approached the newly arrived Paul Andrew, formerly Peter Ainsworth, in Toner's Bar in Dublin for the next stage of his "rebirth" was a complete stranger and took the "new" Paul by surprise when he quietly introduced himself. After confirming Paul's identity, he asked him to follow him outside where he led him to a two-year-old silver Ford Mondeo. He opened the boot for Paul's recently bought black backpack containing the few possessions that he had brought from Moelfre and then Paul got in the front passenger seat. Donal, his new driver, got in, started the engine, and they set off on the journey to meet Jerry in Belfast and the start of his new life.

The two-hour journey seemed to pass very quickly for Paul. Donal was not the most talkative of people which suited Paul fine. He was happy admiring the scenery as he kept replaying the last couple of weeks over and over in his mind, reliving every detail and still marvelling at how smoothly it had all gone. He could not imagine what must be going on back at Wade's after his disappearance and the loss of their latest consignment of gems. They would be frantically trying to figure out what had happened and would certainly have been less convinced by the staged disappearance than the police – they knew very well what the motive for it was, whereas the police knew nothing about the large consignment of missing gemstones. He was sure that the people behind the smuggling ring would be very suspicious of his convenient disappearance and would probably suspect that he may well have been involved, he just hoped that they would finally come to believe that there had been a falling out between him and his accomplices and that he had paid the penalty. They would no doubt continue the search for the gemstones to see if they surfaced on the black market, but if they did eventually come across them, he hoped he would be completely lost in his new identity and life in a different country. He was sure the police, on the other hand, would lose interest quite quickly: all they knew was that a courier driver for a reputable Manchester company had disappeared in suspicious circumstances. He knew they would not get any help from Wade's for obvious reasons – so although they might believe there was more to it, with nothing to go on, his hope was that the investigation would peter out to just another unsolved missing persons case.

Paul and Donal finally arrived at a small detached three-bedroom house on the outskirts of Belfast where Jerry Duggan was waiting for them. Donal saw Paul to the door and then returned to the Mondeo and drove off. Jerry walked up to Paul and gave him a big warm bear hug in greeting.

"How are you Pete – sorry, Paul? Great to see you. Everything OK?" asked Jerry with a big smile on his face. "It went well didn't it, everything to plan? I'll bet the people at Wade's are really brassed off with you!"

Paul just stood there smiling – he thought he was going to burst into tears but he managed to control himself. He still couldn't believe it had all happened and he was free and away.

"You'll stay here tonight and then I'll take you to a staging house in Ballyclare, it's about thirteen miles from here, out towards Larne. You'll stay there for a few weeks and Mick and Aileen will look after you. They'll go back over to Anglesey a couple of times and show their faces at the two rentals as well, just to cover their tracks. We'll set you up with a bit of work doing some driving and delivery work initially until we can find you something permanent, that OK with you? The £10,000 is in your new account and we'll put the rest in when we've sold the stones. You were right about them, our initial estimate is we should get close to £200,000. We're putting them through a few different dealers, we don't want to attract any attention from your friends across the water do we?" laughed Jerry. "You settle down and relax, help yourself to anything in the kitchen. There's tea and coffee and food in the fridge. I've got to nip out to sort a few things out. I should be back in a couple of hours." With that, Jerry put on a brown leather bomber jacket, picked up his keys, went out, locked the front door and got into his silver Audi RS3, the same one that he had used when he had picked Paul up in Manchester at their first meeting.

Two hours later, Jerry returned with an assortment of Chinese take-away food.

"Hope you like Chinese," he announced, putting the cartons down on the kitchen table. "Fancy a beer with it? I've got a few bottles of Stella if you like," Jerry said as he retrieved two large bottles from the fridge.

"Love it thanks, and I'll have a bottle too please," Paul replied.

So they sat at the table and ate the food and drank the chilled lager. Paul tried to question Jerry about his new life between each mouthful of Chinese food, asking where he was going to live and what it was like there. But Jerry told him to enjoy his meal and he would go through all that later and in more detail when they got to the house at Ballyclare.

Shortly after finishing the meal, Jerry once again gave his apologies about not being able to stay and chat. He took Paul upstairs and showed him his room and then left again saying he would be back later and suggesting Paul go to bed when he was ready as they would have an early start.

About eleven o'clock, Paul finally gave up waiting for Jerry to return and went to bed; it had been an exceedingly long and eventful day and he soon drifted off into a deep, dreamless sleep.

What seemed like two minutes later Paul was being shaken awake by Jerry.

"Come on, it's time to get up. Have a shower if you want, I'll see you downstairs."

Paul looked sleepily at the clock by the side of his bed which said 6.35am. He got up, showered, dressed and went down to the kitchen where Jerry was sitting at the table with a large mug of freshly brewed coffee.

"Kettle's brewed, there's tea and coffee and milk in the fridge. Have a cup if you want, we'll get some breakfast later OK?" Jerry said.

Paul made himself a cup of tea and joined him at the table. "What's the plan Jerry?" he asked.

"When we've finished these, I'll drive you over to Ballyclare to Mick and Aileen's place. As I said, they will look after you until your new place is ready. It's a big farmhouse about a mile out of the town, well away from prying eyes, you'll be fine there."

They finished their drinks in silence and then Paul retrieved his backpack from the bedroom and they went out to the car. Jerry drove Paul to the farmhouse, which was a large stone single storey building with several barns and outhouses dotted around. The house itself was approached down quite a long, winding unpaved lane and could not be seen from the road. Mick and Aileen were waiting by the door as they approached as Jerry had called them just before turning off the main road to warn them of their arrival. There were brief introductions and then they all went inside.

"I'm off," said Jerry shortly afterwards. "Mick and Aileen will look after you and I'll see you later." With that, Jerry left, got in the Audi and disappeared back down the lane.

"Right," Mick said, "a quick tour of the farm and I'll show you where everything is Paul."

He started with Paul's room where he left his backpack and then through the main living areas and into the kitchen where Aileen was busy preparing some kind of stew on the range.

"Now outside, I'll show you where we keep the cars and the one you'll have the use of." At that, Mick led him out of the kitchen across the paved back yard and into a large stone barn with a wide tarmacked surface leading from the entrance to the lane which joined the main road. There were three vehicles parked inside, a large black Range Rover Sport with tinted black windows, a silver Audi Estate and a blue Ford Focus.

"I don't suppose mine is the Range Rover, Mick?" joked Paul as he walked towards the Ford Focus. Those were the last words that Paul Andrews/Peter Ainsworth uttered before the 9mm bullet from the Sig Sauer P238 entered the back of his head, just where the neck joins the base of the skull. He died instantaneously and slumped to the ground. Aileen joined Mick moments later carrying Paul/Peter's backpack and helped to carry the inert corpse out of the back of the barn where to a recently dug grave about thirty metres into the field. They dropped him in, along with his new backpack and everything relating to his new identity, and poured the contents of a large bag of lime over the body. Once they had shovelled the freshly dug earth back into the grave, Paul Andrews/Peter Ainsworth truly had disappeared.

A couple of hours later, Jerry Duggan was sitting at his laptop and digitally transferring the £10,000 out of the account of Paul Andrews into another fictitious person's account; three wire transfers later, it was back in the offshore account from where it had originated a week earlier.

PART TWO

Chapter 2

"You shouldn't be sticking your nose into things that don't concern you, forget about Plas Meirion or you will regret it."

The text arrived completely out of the blue at 4.13pm on Tuesday 30th October 2018 while Steve Guest was enjoying a quiet hour re-reading one of his favourite John Grisham novels. He had only recently returned from a walk along the coastal path between Moelfre and Benllech on the beautiful island of Anglesey where he and his wife Carla had retired to almost eight months ago from their long-time home in Ramsbottom in Lancashire. His first thoughts were "What things? Who the hell sent this and how did they get my number?" Once he had gotten over the initial shock, he immediately sent his own text to his new friend and "partner in crime" retired Detective Chief Inspector John Wyn Thomas, formerly of North Wales CID: "Meet me at the pub tonight around 8pm, we need to talk."

It had all started about a month ago when Steve overheard a conversation at the bar of his new local pub one Friday evening. He was enjoying his first pint and had been mulling over for the umpteenth time what he could do to occupy all the newly acquired free time now that he was officially and finally "retired". Nothing had sprung to mind and nor had he had any flashes of inspiration when two locals he was on nodding terms with started chatting about "that business down at Plas Meirion" and "what a waste that the bungalow is just sitting there empty with such fabulous views over the bay, being left to rot away" and how "with some work, it would make a great home for someone". Steve's ears had pricked up at that. Tom Clarke, one of his former golf partners back at his local golf club in Lancashire, was the owner of a builders and property developers; on learning of Steve's impending move down to Anglesey, he'd asked him to keep an eye out for any possible refurbishment opportunities on the island.

Steve had got off his stool, moved round the bar to them and said, "Evening gents, sorry to interrupt, I'm Steve Guest. I moved into the area earlier in the year and I couldn't help but overhear you talking about a bungalow that would make someone a great home. I have a friend who specialises in renovations and that sort of thing and he might be interested in having a look at it."

The one nearest to Steve, a small, wiry, grey-haired individual with tanned face and hands, replied, "Evening, I'm Andy Griffiths and this is my mate Bernie, glad to meet you. We've seen you in here before haven't we?"

"Yes, I usually come in on a Friday night about this time now that the season is over and most of the holiday makers have left!"

"Yes, it gets really full in July and August, even during the week," Andy confirmed. "We've been coming in here for over 20 years and it's always been the same, it's a popular place. I would forget about Plas Meirion though if I were you. It's been unoccupied since all that trouble a year ago. It was the anniversary this week of that lad's disappearance, Peter Ainsworth he was called, that's why we were talking about it."

"What trouble?" asked Steve. "We've been coming down to the island regularly for years although mostly on the West coast round Rhosneigr way and I don't remember anything about it."

"It was all over the *Anglesey Guardian* and social media for a couple of weeks but it was off-season fortunately for the tourist trade, so it probably didn't create as much of a stir as it might have done," Bernie chipped in.

"Yes," Andy continued. "They never did find out what happened there, what with the blood and the guy just disappearing. No one here really knew anything about him, he only lived there for about eight months, he never came into the village and seemed to keep to himself. The bungalow is about half a mile out of here, off the road that leads to the A5025 to Amlwch, down at the end of a narrow country lane which eventually leads down to the coastal path and the sea. The lane itself doesn't go anywhere except to the house and you can't see it from the main road. He had a white Transit van which was pretty new from memory and he came and went at all times apparently. Sometimes back through here, going towards Bangor and the mainland, and sometimes going the other way, towards Amlwch and perhaps to Holyhead or using the ferries to Ireland. Even the local estate agents Davies & Co who handled the original sale couldn't shed much light on his identity. Apparently everything was done through a solicitor's office in Manchester and they handled all the paperwork and the actual letting. It was an unusual setup according to the local paper, the estate agent just provided a management service for the property – cleaners and regular inspections, that sort of thing. You could ask at Davies & Co, they have their office in Llangefni, perhaps they might be able to help but I doubt it."

"Thanks for that guys, fancy a pint?" Steve asked.

"No thanks Steve, we're off. Perhaps next time," Andy said as they got up to leave. Just as they were going through the door, Bernie turned round and called, "If you are interested in finding out more about what went on, come here during the week, try a Tuesday or a Wednesday. John Wyn Thomas comes in most weeks one of those days, he's a big guy, short grey hair and beard, over six foot tall, you can't miss him. Ex-Detective Chief Inspector, he was in charge of the case at the time, in fact I think it was his last before he retired. See you."

Steve could not believe his luck – he had found something to get his teeth into, two things in fact. He had always fancied himself as bit of an amateur sleuth, based on nothing other than his love of puzzles especially crosswords, just like his favourite television detective, although he had always done *The Daily Telegraph*'s cryptic one as their sports pages were much better than *The Times*'s in his opinion. He was also an avid reader of detective and crime thriller novels. He thought that perhaps after solving the mystery of whatever happened at Plas Meirion there might be the possibility of a house refurbishment project with his pal Tom Clarke to put the icing on the cake, not to mention a few pounds in his pocket. Tom was an old golf partner from when he was a member at Brownhill Golf Club back when he lived in Ramsbottom. Tom had his own small building company which specialised in renovating and refurbishing old houses and he'd asked Steve to keep an eye out for any projects on Anglesey which could be converted into holiday lets or for re-sale, knowing that Anglesey was such a popular holiday destination.

As he sat at the bar, Steve pulled out the small notebook and pen he always carried and thought about his plan of action.

First, he thought, visit the estate agents in Llangefni, although he was not overly optimistic about anything useful coming out of that based on what Andy and Bernie had said. Secondly, and much more interestingly, try to meet up with the ex-Detective Chief Inspector in the pub and thirdly, try and speak to the solicitors to see if he could find out more about the house and the refurbishment possibility.

As expected, the visit to the estate agents the following Monday produced nothing of interest except a confirmation that it had been an unusual arrangement in that they only provided the cleaners and regular inspections. All the rent and money matters were dealt with directly by the solicitors. If he wanted any information regarding the property and any potential purchase, they confirmed he would need to contact the solicitors in Manchester, a firm called Jonathon T Underwood Solicitors. They also volunteered the fact that they had never spoken to the solicitor directly, they had always dealt with his office manager, a Mrs Tricia Scott.

As Steve had expected, the visit was a dead end but, as suggested, he decided he would try and speak to the solicitors but not until after a chat with John Wyn Thomas at the pub when hopefully he would learn a lot more about what had happened at the house.

It was on his second Tuesday evening visit after one other fruitless Wednesday evening call to the pub that Steve eventually "bumped" into his quarry and struck up a casual conversation with the retired Detective Chief Inspector, a conversation which proved far more informative.

Chapter 3

When Steve walked into the pub, John Wyn Thomas was sitting on his own at a table in the corner by the large panoramic window which overlooked the bay, his usual place as Steve came to know.

Steve went up to the bar and ordered a pint of lager; having taken a quick taste, he wandered over to John's table.

"Mind if I join you?" Steve asked. "Is it John Wyn Thomas?" he continued.

"It is and you are?" John replied abruptly with a hint of a frown; he was obviously not happy about complete strangers approaching him which was not surprising given his previous occupation.

"My name is Steve Guest, I recently retired down here from Lancashire with my wife Carla from a place called Ramsbottom, don't know if you've heard of it?"

"Yes, an ex-colleague of mine came from over that way," John replied.

"I was chatting to a couple of locals in here recently, Andy Griffiths and his mate Bernie, do you know them?" continued Steve.

"I do."

"Well, they were sat at the bar reminiscing about a bungalow near here called Plas Meirion and a bit of a mystery that surrounded it a while ago. We got talking and they suggested I have a word with you about it."

"They did, did they. And what is your interest in Plas Meirion?" John asked.

"I have a good friend who does house renovations and refurbishments, that sort of thing, and he asked me to keep an eye out for any possible projects when I moved down here," Steve replied, masking the real reason he was interested in the mystery. "Andy mentioned that it seemed such a waste that the bungalow had been left empty since the disappearance of that guy, Peter Ainsworth I think they said he was called, and I said I would be interested in having a look at it. That's when they suggested I have a chat with you as you would know as much about the house and what went on as anyone."

"Andy no doubt also told you we never found Pete Ainsworth or discovered what happened at Plas Meirion and I retired shortly afterwards. It was a complete mystery to all of us. The company he worked for, Wade's, and the solicitors who handled the letting of the bungalow for them were not in the least bit helpful at the time. We had our suspicions that something was not quite right with the whole incident and my sergeant did a thorough check on both the operations of Wade's, the lad's employers, and their solicitors but he found nothing. As far as I know, the case is still open but since I left the force I don't think there have been any new developments. My old detective sergeant, who did most of the legwork and questioning, is still at Colwyn Bay and we meet up now and again for a pint and a chat but he has never mentioned any developments so I assume it has just remained an open "Missing Persons" file. It wasn't how I wanted to leave, with an unsolved case hanging over me, but that's how it goes."

Steve took another drink and then continued. "I'd like to find out more about the bungalow and see if there is a possible property development opportunity. You never know, I might stumble across something about that lad's disappearance in the process," he said, although of course it was Peter Ainsworth's disappearance that he was mainly interested in. "I understand that a Manchester solicitor handled the bungalow letting so I think I'll give them a call. Perhaps next time you see your old detective sergeant you could ask him about it for me, tell him about my interest in the bungalow in case there is something he knows which could help me," Steve added, more in hope than expectation.

"I wouldn't be too optimistic if I were you, but give me a contact number and if I remember next time I see Charlie I'll have a word for you. I must admit I would be interested myself to see if they have found out anything further about what happened. At the time, I was just happy to leave and probably didn't give it my fullest attention – as I said, I left most of the legwork and interviews to my detective sergeant. It has always rankled that I finished on such a high-profile unsolved case."

Steve gave John his mobile number, finished his pint and left the pub, resolving to ring the solicitor first thing in the morning.

At 9.30am the following day, Steve rang the office of Jonathon T Underwood LLB (Hons), a sole practitioner based on West Mosely Street, just off Piccadilly in the centre of Manchester.

"Good morning, Underwood's Solicitors, how may I help you?" came the polite greeting.

"Hi, my name is Steve Guest. Could I make an appointment to see Mr Underwood please?"

"May I ask what it is regarding?" the well-spoken but firm female voice replied.

"Yes, I am looking to buy a house and I was hoping to engage Mr Underwood for the legal side of things."

"I'm sorry but Mr Underwood doesn't get involved in general practice, he only works for a small number of retained clients. Perhaps I could recommend another firm?" she replied courteously.

"It's just that I was told that I should contact Mr Underwood by Davies & Co, an estate agents in Llangefni. It's regarding Plas Meirion at Moelfre on Anglesey and they informed me that he was the solicitor who had handled that property in the past," Steve persisted.

"What is your interest in the property Mr Guest?" the voice on the other end of the line asked, now sounding decidedly frosty.

"As I told the estate agents, I'm looking into the possibility of perhaps buying the property for a development project. I understand it has been empty for a while," Steve continued.

"I am afraid you have been misinformed Mr Guest, Plas Meirion is not for sale. It is owned by one of Mr Underwood's retained clients and, as it happens, I believe it will be occupied again in the very near future. Sorry you have wasted your time." And with that, the lady abruptly hung up before Steve could ask any more questions.

Steve called John Wyn Thomas to update him on his fruitless call to Underwood's and inform him of the impending arrival of a new occupant for Plas Meirion. John expressed no surprise at the lack of help from the solicitor but was extremely interested in the potential new development if it turned out that Plas Meirion was indeed to receive a new resident.

"I'll give Charlie a call and arrange to meet up. I wonder if he knows anything about this and if so who the new tenant is and if he is another employee of Wade's, or if they have sold it. As far as I know, it's not been on the market for sale or to rent. I'll give you a call if I find out anything of interest," John replied.

With that, they hung up and, as Steve could not advance his enquiries any further, he waited for John to get back to him, hopefully with some news.

It was two weeks before John called Steve back and informed him that he had met up with his former detective sergeant for a drink and had asked him off the record if there had been any new developments in the investigation into Peter Ainsworth's disappearance. After being told no, he had informed his old DS about the impending new resident at

Plas Meirion. Charlie did tell him that they had been keeping an eye on both Wade's and the solicitor but there seemed to be nothing suspicious going on at either firm and then he had asked John how he knew about Plas Meirion's new tenant, which he said was certainly news to him. John told Steve that he had kept his reply vague and that he had told him that someone he had met at his local in Moelfre had mentioned something about a potential refurbishment project at Plas Meirion but that when he had approached the solicitor he had been informed about the new resident, killing his development plans. John said that Charlie had thanked him for letting him know, said that he would keep a closer eye on things over on Anglesey just in case there were any new leads and asked John to let him know if he or his new friend heard anything out of the ordinary about the house or its new tenant.

On an impulse, Steve decided to invite John over for a meal at their bungalow, hoping to get to know him better and perhaps, through him, to get more involved in the local community. Steve and Carla had been on the island for nearly a year and had made very few new friends. John readily accepted as he had become a bit of a loner since his retirement and so they arranged to meet up on the following Saturday evening. Steve asked if spaghetti bolognese would be OK and John confirmed that would be fine.

The retired Chief Inspector arrived promptly at 7pm and handed Steve a bottle of Merlot as they shook hands and went through to the living room where Steve's wife Carla was already seated on the two-seater sofa. Steve introduced John and Carla and took the wine through to the kitchen as John sat down in one of the two armchairs which matched the two-tone stone-coloured, herringbone design sofa.

"How are you settling into your new home here on Anglesey, Carla?" said John, opening the conversation.

"Very well thanks, John. I don't know if Steve mentioned it but we had a static caravan over at Rhosneigr for several years before we came down to live so we already knew the island very well. We loved coming down for long weekends and the odd week two or three times a year and always intended to move down permanently when we retired. Have you lived here long?"

"Not much longer than yourselves actually. I bought my bungalow here in Moelfre when I retired just under two years ago. Before that, I lived in Colwyn Bay where I was stationed at the Police Headquarters for the best part of twenty years. I was born and spent most of my early life in Abergele just up the coast before joining the force straight from school," replied John as Steve returned from the kitchen and sat in the other armchair in front of the large bay window which had a spectacular panoramic view of the bay and out to Snowdonia and the Great Orme at Llandudno in the distance.

"Do you have any family John?" continued Carla.

"No," John answered. "I'm divorced and we didn't have any children."

"Oh, I am sorry John."

"It's fine Carla, it was a while ago now. We married young and Alice never really got used to being a copper's wife and not having any children made it less of a wrench for both of us. She remarried a few years later and they have two or three children now, they live in Prestatyn I think. How about you and Steve, do you have any kids?" John asked, steering the conversation away from his personal life which had been mainly one of regret, failed relationships and loneliness away from the police force.

"Yes we have two, a boy and girl, both grown up and flown the nest. Simon is in the army, the Intelligence Corps, stationed in Germany at the moment, and Charlotte is married with a young girl, Janis, and lives with her husband Greg down near Oxford. We don't get to see them much, they have their own lives now. Excuse me and I'll go and finish getting the meal ready, should be about ten minutes." With that, Carla left the two men and went through the dining area into the kitchen.

Steve stood up. "Do you want a drink John? We have beer, cans only I'm afraid, or red or white wine?"

"I'm alright thanks for now, I'll have some red with the meal," John answered. "Steve, why don't you tell me a bit about yourself and Carla? You've had my brief biography, what did you do before retiring down here?"

"OK, let's see. I was born and brought up in a place called Hyde, don't know if you've heard of it? Famous for Dr Shipley, the Moor's Murderers and the biggest loss in an FA Cup match, twenty-six nil to Preston North End. Although recently we have had someone we are justly proud of – Ricky "The Hitman" Hatton comes from Hyde, an ex-world champion and great boxer. His younger brother Matthew was no slouch either, I think he was a European Champion as well. They still live there as far as I know and Ricky opened a boxing and fitness gym at the top of Market Street when he retired.

"I went to the local grammar school, great place and teachers, loved every minute of it. Went to college in Leeds which was a complete waste of time as it turned out. I was on the dole for a while after I left and had no idea what I wanted to do. My degree was in Construction Management, it was a four-year sandwich course and I spent my year in industry as a trainee site engineer for John Laing's on a couple of multistorey office developments in Manchester. That only served to convince me that I definitely did not want a career in the construction industry, although I did enjoy working on the sites. I finally drifted into a sales job for a building fixings company, the main attraction being that they supplied a car. I did that for a couple of years before trying different sales job, selling insurance, advertising space and then with Rank Xerox selling their new range of word processors – this was well before computers and laptops. The sales training with Xerox was brilliant and after that I went from strength to strength, firstly in telecommunications and then the new mobile phone industry and finally the online auction marketplace.

"I played cricket in summer, which was my true passion, and squash in winter until old age and infirmity caught up with me and now I play a bit of golf and we do quite a bit of walking. I met Carla at one of the firms we both worked at and married her three years later. We have been married for thirty-seven years and, as Carla said earlier, we have two children. Before we married, I was living in a flat in Cheetham Hill in Manchester and Carla was living at home with her mum and dad in Moston in Manchester. Our first house together was near Gig Lane in Bury and then we moved out to Ramsbottom. We lived around that area until we retired down here earlier this year. I think that's about it for me."

"Wow, that was pretty comprehensive Steve! Did you rehearse that before I arrived?" joked John.

They continued chatting about things in general, the staple topics of the dire state of the country, politics and society. They had just got on to sport but as Steve was a big Manchester City fan and John's interest was only in rugby that was about to end quickly when luckily Carla called through to them, "The food is on the table, come and get it."

They joined Carla at the table and started what turned into a very enjoyable evening for the three new friends.

John said his farewells just after 11pm and they agreed to keep in touch and meet up now and again at the pub, but as far as Plas Meirion was concerned they agreed it was as far as they could take it.

Steve, however, had no intention of letting his investigation drop and decided to keep a close eye on the mystery bungalow. He was convinced there was a lot more to it than just a simple missing persons case and he was determined to find out what had actually happened to Peter Ainsworth and what it was really all about.

Chapter 4

Twelve months before Steve Guest received that mysterious text, in the first week of October 2017, Peter Ainsworth had been sitting in Toner's on Baggot Street in Dublin at 2pm as arranged, at the start of a new life, drinking his first pint of Guinness as Paul Andrews which seemed to taste even better than usual. He had £10,000 in a bank account in his new name of Paul Andrews with another £10,000 to come once the stones had been sold. He could have had any name he wanted but for some strange reason he decided to keep his initials. It had all gone like a dream, just as he and Jerry had planned.

He had met Jerry by accident in the exercise yard at Strangeways about fourteen months earlier, shortly before he was due to be released after serving his two-year sentence for robbing someone at the National Westminster Bank cash point next to Gregg's in Salford Precinct. Pete had not planned it, he was going to Gregg's for a meat and potato pasty for his lunch and the guy had just withdrawn £200 from the ATM and was absentmindedly checking the cash as he turned in to Pete. The next thing he knew, Pete had hit him in the face, grabbed the notes and sprinted round the corner, stuffing the money into his pocket as he went. Unfortunately for Pete, when he hit the startled man he had cut his knuckles on the guy's teeth, two of which he broke, leaving a perfect sample of his DNA which, when combined with the CCTV from the precinct cameras and his comprehensive juvenile file, made the task of finding and arresting him relatively simple. His only option was to plead guilty which, because of his many prior offences, earned him his first senior custodial sentence in Strangeways.

Jerry Duggan, on the other hand, was a hardened career criminal from Belfast nearing the end of a lengthy sentence for armed robbery resulting from an attack on a security van by Jerry and three others, all carrying firearms – two sawn-off shotguns, a 9mm Luger Semi-Automatic Pistol and AK 47 assault rifle to be specific – which went terribly wrong thanks to an anonymous tip-off and a waiting SWAT team backed up by several armed officers from the Serious Crimes Squad.

Pete was talking with a fellow inmate called Simon Ashley who had the cell a couple down from his on B wing and with whom he had become good friends after finding out that not only had they been to the same secondary school in Wythenshawe, although Simon was a couple of years older, but they were born on the same estate and both supported Manchester City. Jerry came towards them and called to Simon, whom he obviously knew, "Simon, I need a word."

"No problem Jerry, this is my mate Pete. He's a good lad from my old estate."

Jerry nodded and then walked away towards the edge of the yard in conversation with Simon. A couple of minutes later Simon returned to Pete and said, "Sorry about that, Jerry just wanted me to pass a message on to my uncle when I get out."

"He looked one serious dude Simon, who the hell is he?" Pete asked.

"Not someone you want to get involved with mate, believe me. He knows my Uncle Jim from back in the day when he was involved in some heavy stuff."

Simon was released shortly afterwards and gave Pete his mobile number and they agreed to meet up when Pete was released.

Pete bumped into Jerry a few times in the yard after that, just passed the time of day but they got on OK and the brief chats were quite amicable.

The week before he was due for release in the October of 2016, Pete had an unexpected visit from his mum's brother Harry. His dad had left home before his fifth birthday leaving Harry to help his mum, unsuccessfully, with Pete's upbringing. Harry had never married and was not blessed with strong paternal instincts – in fact, it would be fair to say he didn't have any – and this, combined with a mother who spent the majority of her social security benefits feeding her drug and drink habits, resulted in Pete's very wayward early life. This was why having not seen him for at least a couple of years, Pete was very surprised when Harry turned up, especially as they had never really got on when Harry did try occasionally over the years to interfere in his life. After completing the usual awkward greetings and establishing that each of them was fine, Harry explained his presence at Strangeways.

"I was speaking to your mum a while ago and she was pleading with me to see if I could help out when you got released. I know you haven't had a great time of it over the last few years but there was nothing I could have done, I had enough of my own troubles without getting involved with you. Anyway, something has come up recently that you might be interested in. You won't know but I got a job at Wade's in Trafford Park through an old mate of mine about six months ago, he's the Transport Manager there. They make some really classy sportswear – trainers, tracksuits, tee shirts, that sort of thing, but top-end gear, really expensive. They have a big manufacturing plant and warehouse in Trafford Park and some flash shops in Manchester, London and Dublin over in Ireland."

Pete just sat there nodding, totally amazed, because he knew his uncle was just a small-time crook and the last person anyone would offer a legitimate job to at a respectable company. He had no idea where this was going – he knew it would probably be illegal but he was intrigued so he just kept smiling and nodding.

"Anyway, I might be able to help fix you up with a job at our place. Give me a call when you get out and we'll have a chat. Your mum has my number." And with that, Harry stood up and left.

One month later, the week after Pete was released, he met as arranged with his Uncle Harry at a pub in Trafford Park just a short distance from the head office and factory of Wade Manufacturing Limited. With him was a short, dark-haired, shifty-looking man who looked in his mid to late thirties who Harry introduced as Mr John Bootle, the Transport Manager at Wade's.

"Your uncle has told me all about you, Pete, not had a great time of it by all accounts. Says you are a good lad at heart, know the ropes, can be trusted, and deserve another chance. If you're interested, we need another delivery driver for our shops in London and Dublin. Your Harry has been doing a great job for us since he joined but we are getting so busy he needs some help. You would start on a three-month trial, we'll see how it goes and then take it from there. You would be self-employed, we would supply the van, pay all expenses, and would pay you at £10 an hour for all hours worked including travelling time to and from the factory. What do you say?"

Pete knew that there was something not right about all this, offering him such a good job out of the blue apparently solely on his uncle's say so. But he was intrigued, especially as having Googled Wade's before the meeting he was extremely impressed with what he had seen. 'What the hell?' he thought, he had nothing better to do and he certainly needed the money, so why not?

"Sounds great, Mr Bootle, thanks very much. When do you want me to start?" replied Pete after only a moment's hesitation.

"We will be looking after Christmas, probably mid to late January. I'll have a chat with Harry and we'll sort something out. We'll be in touch." At that, he stood up, shook Pete's hand and left.

"Right, Pete," said Harry, "I'll give you a call." Then Harry also stood up and left the pub.

Nine weeks later, on Monday 17th January 2017, Pete was at the wheel of his brand-new Transit van filled with Wade's designer leisurewear on his first delivery trip to London. Nothing out of the ordinary happened over the next couple of months, he had regular weekly trips to London and Dublin delivering stock to the two shops. He was living at home with his mum in Wythenshawe and, as he was now paying rent, she was more than happy. On Monday mornings he drove into Trafford Park, picked up his load of stock then drove to London and dropped it off at the shop, picked up any returns and stayed overnight at a Travel Inn. Tuesday morning he drove back home to Wythenshawe. On Wednesday morning he drove back to Trafford Park, dropped off any returns, picked up his stock for Dublin and then went back home. Early Thursday mornings he drove to Holyhead and caught the 8.15am Irish Ferries to Dublin, delivered his stock, stayed overnight in Dublin and then caught the early return ferry arriving in Holyhead at 11.30am Friday morning. He then drove to the factory, dropped off any returns and had a meeting with Mr Bootle about his week; he always seemed to be concerned that he was happy, enjoying the job and had no problems, which in itself made Pete feel very uneasy. He knew that something was not right with the whole set-up, it was all too easy, but he had no idea what it was leading to. Wade's was a very respectable, seemingly successful company and although it was all a bit boring, he was earning good money so what the hell. He rarely saw his uncle who seemed to be on the road most of the time, sometimes going to the shops but only occasionally and he had no idea what he was doing or where he was going the rest of the time. At the start of his third probationary month, Pete was finally to find out what it was that he had really been taken on for.

He got the call from Harry on a Sunday morning at 11am asking if he was free that afternoon for a chat. He was and he agreed to go over to his uncle's flat in Didsbury for 3pm. He had not been to the flat before so he was intrigued to see what it was like – probably some grubby little one-bedroom place in one of the many old converted Victorian houses which were home to thousands of students in South Manchester. When he got there he could not have been more wrong. It was situated in a new development complete with a security entrance system. After announcing himself over the intercom for Flat 4 he was buzzed in and when he knocked on the door of the flat on the second floor it was John Bootle who opened the door and ushered him in.

"Afternoon, Pete, thanks for coming, take a seat," John said, pointing at an extremely comfortable, expensive-looking leather armchair. John sat down on the one next to it as his uncle hovered behind the even more luxurious matching three-seater sofa.

"Very impressive, Uncle, didn't realise you were doing so well," Pete said with perhaps a little too much sarcasm and a trace of anger in his voice. "Does Mum know about this place?" he asked, knowing full well the answer.

"This isn't Harry's, he just lives here, Pete, it is owned by Wade's. You could call it a perk for loyal service to the company," Bootle said with a sly smile. "That is what we are here to discuss. We would like to offer you an opportunity to enjoy the same, shall we say, benefits that Harry enjoys. It involves quite a big change in your present living circumstances; your duties would remain broadly similar, but the rewards could be substantially more. Interested?"

"Definitely, Mr Bootle," Pete said without hesitation. 'Now we're getting to it,' he thought.

"Good lad. The first thing you would have to do is move out of your mum's and into a house on the East coast of Anglesey, a place called Moelfre. It's a bungalow actually owned by Wade's, although their name doesn't appear on the paperwork related to the place for tax reasons. It's fully furnished of course, not quite as flash as this but very comfortable with everything you would need. Officially you will be renting it on a long-term let through a solicitor here in Manchester and it is managed by a local estate agents based at Llangefni. It won't actually cost you anything but you need to appear to be the tenant. Once down there you will carry on your deliveries to Dublin through Holyhead, but twice a week instead of once, and of course you will kick the London trips into touch. After a while, when you have fully settled in with your new routine, a package will be delivered to you about once a month at Moelfre. You will then bring it to me at Trafford Park when you come in to pick up the stock for your next trip to Dublin. You will get a cash bonus of £1,000 for each package, paid to you immediately when you hand it over to me at the factory. I'm sure I don't have to tell you that this delivery is completely off the books and you are not to mention anything about it to anyone. Still interested?"

Pete sat quietly for a short time. He had known from the outset that it was bound to be something illegal, something involving deliveries, but this had taken him completely by surprise. He had presumed it was perhaps some under-the-counter trainers or dodgy designer gear but this seemed to be something much more serious, especially as it involved moving to a new house and to the coast as well. This smelt of drugs and he was not too sure he wanted to get involved with something as heavy as that. On the other hand, he got to live by the sea, something he had always dreamt about, in his own place, free of charge, and earn at least an extra grand a month tax free in his pocket. 'What the hell?' he thought once again. 'Go for it.'

"Count me in, Mr Bootle," Pete finally confirmed after a few moment's thought.

"Excellent Pete, I'll leave Harry to fill in the details. See you soon."

When Bootle left, Pete looked at Harry. "What is it, Uncle? It's not drugs is it?"

"You don't need to know but you can take my word it's not drugs, OK?"

Although not totally convinced (he knew how much his uncle's word was worth), Pete felt a bit happier. Harry told him all the things he needed to know about his new job and helped him move down to Moelfre over the next several days.

Pete soon adjusted to his new surroundings and quickly settled into the new home and routine. His rearranged itinerary consisted of driving to Manchester on Monday morning, picking up his first Dublin load and driving back to Moelfre. On Tuesday, he took the early ferry from Holyhead to Dublin, drove to the store, dropped off the stock, got the last ferry back to Holyhead and drove back home to Moelfre in the evening. Wednesday morning he went into Manchester again, picked up the stock and then back to Moelfre. Thursday, early ferry to Dublin again, drove to the store, dropped off the stock, then the ferry back to Moelfre. Then finally on Friday morning, into Manchester for his weekly 11am meeting with John Bootle, then home for the weekend.

He slowly got to know the local area and settled into his new life, very much keeping to himself. The bungalow was about half a mile out of what used to be the small fishing village of Moelfre. It was out of sight at the end of a narrow winding road off the main A5025 between Amlwch and Benllech, directly overlooking the bay and now an area very popular with holiday makers throughout the year with lots of holiday lets and static caravan and second-home owners. It was ideal if you were someone who wanted to remain anonymous amongst a constantly changing holiday population. There was another bungalow halfway down the lane between Pete's place and the main road but it was a short-term holiday let and the residents constantly changed, usually weekly or fortnightly. The only other people who came down their road were the cleaners who serviced both properties and were contracted through the estate agents in Llangefni, monthly in Pete's bungalow's case and on each turnaround of holiday makers in the holiday let, plus the odd hiker on their way down to the coastal path. He spent most of his spare time either on the beaches at Benllech, Traeth Bychan or Lligwy, or exploring the island, especially the coastal path which was about 140 miles long and went right round the entire island of Anglesey.

About six weeks into his new job, he finally got notification of his first "delivery" by text from a withheld number to the PAYG phone his uncle had given to him along with a laptop and company smart phone. The message simply said, 'Package to arrive soon' and was the first communication he had received on it, although he had been told, like his company phone, to have it switched on at all times. He felt a strange thrill of excitement that he was at last going to find out what was involved in his new job and perhaps what all the detailed and expensive preparations were for, not to mention the promise of £1,000 in cash for himself. He knew not to reply and simply waited for further instructions.

They duly arrived on the PAYG phone on the Saturday five days later. 'Package will be delivered next Tuesday night between midnight and 6am Wednesday morning.' Sure enough, at about 4am on the following Wednesday morning, someone rang the bell at the back door and then disappeared back into the night, presumably going down the small private path which led from the back of the bungalow to the coast path. Pete had been sat in his favourite armchair all night, wide awake with excited anticipation and the help of four cups of coffee. He waited five minutes as instructed and then went to the back door and retrieved the package. It was about nine inches long by four inches in diameter, a plain black cylindrical plastic container with a sealed top and bottom. It was quite heavy for its size and felt full of whatever was in it; it was well packed and did not make any sound when Pete gently shook it. Whatever he had imagined it would be, and he had spent a lot of time wondering, this was not it. He spent the next couple of hours puzzling over what could possibly be inside and dozing on and off before finally giving up, having a shower, getting dressed and setting off to Manchester for his regular Wednesday pick up but this time with the new mystery package.

He arrived at the factory and went straight to John Bootle's office as arranged with the package in his new rucksack which hung loosely over his left shoulder.

"Morning, Pete," the Transport Manager said as he stood up from behind his desk and closed the door as Pete sat down in the chair across from his own. "Everything go OK in Dublin?"

"Yes thanks, Mr Bootle, everything was fine. Brought a few returns back," replied Pete as he put his rucksack on the floor between his chair and the desk. After discussing the uneventful trip for a couple of minutes, Pete wrapped up their pre-arranged dialogue just in case they were overheard. "Is it OK if I pop down to the warehouse to sort out the returns, Mr Bootle?"

"Sure, no problem, see you before you go." At which point, Pete stood up, leaving the rucksack on the floor, and left the office. Before he had gone many paces from the office door, Bootle had quickly removed the cylinder from the rucksack, put it in the top drawer of his desk and replaced it with a brown A4 envelope containing £1,000 in used £20 notes. The Transport Manager then picked up the bag, went to the office door and, holding it up, called to Pete, "You've left your bag Pete."

"Sorry, Mr Bootle," said Pete, retrieving his bag from his boss and going down to the warehouse to sort out the returns.

After the fourth successful delivery, Pete's curiosity over the contents of the packages, which were always identical and always delivered in the same way, was becoming unbearable. He knew he should leave well alone and keep pocketing the money and asking no questions but he couldn't. He had to try and find out what he was delivering to John Bootle once a month and where it was coming from and especially why they were prepared to pay an additional £1,000 for the simple task of delivering it to Manchester which, as far as he could see, was pretty risk free. It was obvious from the specific location of the bungalow and time of the deliveries that they must be coming from somewhere at sea or they were using a boat to transport them from further along the coast somewhere. He knew the guy always went down the path behind the house towards the sea but that was it. He had always waited five minutes after the bell was rung before retrieving the package from the back door, as instructed by John Bootle, giving the delivery man plenty of time to disappear back into the dark.

For the next delivery, Pete decided that he would find somewhere to hide-out far enough away from the path that the guy could not possibly stumble across him but close enough to see where he went. To help him in his plan, he ordered some night vision binoculars through the internet which duly arrived five days later. He found the perfect place to hide on some elevated ground about fifty metres away to the right of the house, between it and the cliff edge above the sea. There was a long trench-like depression about two metres wide and half a metre deep running down towards the sea which he could lie flat in and be invisible to anyone walking up the path behind the house to the back door and it gave him a clear view all around the bungalow and down to the sea. There were also no paths near to his proposed hideout which anyone, including the delivery man, could come down and accidentally discover him. He knew it was risky but he was ready and determined to go ahead with his plan. Now all he needed was another delivery.

He did not have long to wait. The first text message arrived the following Monday as usual announcing the imminent arrival, followed by the confirmatory email on the Saturday for the delivery the following Tuesday night/Wednesday morning. He was all set and just hoped for decent weather – he didn't fancy lying in the pouring rain for several hours because the deliveries so far had been done between 1am and 4am and he would have to be in position well before midnight in case they came early and be prepared to be there certainly until it started getting light.

The following Tuesday evening he was in position by 11pm. After a couple of trial stakeouts, he had made it as comfortable as possible for himself by using a dark blue, semi-inflated beach airbed – it was the darkest colour he could find. He found that when he lay on it, he was still below the level of the edge of the gulley and could easily raise his head above it for a clear view all around.

Fortunately, as forecast, the weather was fine, cold but dry. He was well wrapped up and had developed a regular stretching and bending routine which kept him hidden but prevented him stiffening up too much. He was also extremely fortunate that the delivery man came reasonably early, just after 1.30am on the Wednesday morning. Pete's first indication of his arrival was the low, muffled noise that sounded like an outboard motor over to his right although when he looked he couldn't see anything. Shortly afterwards, the motor stopped and there was silence. Then a few minutes later Pete saw him through his night vision binoculars come up from the edge of the cliffs where the path started. So he was right that he had come by boat – but from which direction? When he first heard the boat he had looked towards the muffled sound, his right, towards Moelfre and Benllech but had seen nothing so perhaps the man had come from the other direction towards Lligwy Bay and Amlwch.

The delivery man walked slowly, carefully picking his way in the dark. He didn't have a torch but the sky was pretty clear and the stars were shining brightly, helping to light his way along the narrow winding path. The man was quite small, dressed in dark-coloured trousers and a long dark three-quarter length coat and was wearing what looked like some kind of dark, tight-fitting head gear. He reached the back door, took the familiar cylinder out of what must have been a large pocket inside his coat and put it on the doorstep as usual. He rang the bell and, after a quick look round, returned down the path towards the coast.

'Right,' thought Pete, 'let's see where you go matey.' He stayed perfectly still and followed him using the binoculars as he went along the path and disappeared out of his vision down towards the sea. Shortly afterwards, Pete heard the motor start up and looked to his left hoping to see the boat as it appeared round the headland going towards Lligwy but nothing appeared; he quickly moved back to his right towards Moelfre in case he had just missed it first time round but still nothing. He started to panic as the sound of the motor was slowly disappearing and obviously getting further away but as he swung back round to his left he just caught sight of what looked like a small rubber dinghy with an outboard motor and two men in it, right on the edge of his periphery vision. It was not going left towards Lligwy and Amlwch but straight out to sea towards one of the many large ships that are often anchored in the Bay off Moelfre before they head on up to

Liverpool to unload their cargo of containers or visit the refineries at Runcorn. He made a mental note of the position of the ship they returned to and, in the morning, using his normal binoculars as he stood on the coastal path above the shingle beach, he had no trouble in making a note of its name.

By the time he had driven into Manchester, delivered the package, picked up his load for Dublin (and of course his £1,000 cash), driven back to Moelfre, showered, had his evening meal, thanks to several visits to Google throughout the day he now knew that the *MV Caracas* had left the port of Lagos, Nigeria, ten days earlier, bound for, amongst other destinations, Liverpool, England. So the question was: what would you expect to be illicitly smuggled out of Nigeria, small enough to fit in a 9x4 inch cylindrical tube but worth all this hassle and investment? You did not have to be a mastermind to answer that he thought – precious gemstones. Apparently, again according to Google, Nigeria was awash with them: diamonds, tourmaline (he had never heard of that one), sapphires, emeralds, amethysts – you name it, they have it. Plus, according to one article he read, Nigeria loses in excess of $3 billion to illegal gemstone trading every year. Well now Pete knew where some of that $3 billion was ending up – at Wade Manufacturing Limited in Trafford Park, Manchester, England.

'But what to do with the information?' thought Peter. He now realised the risks he was running were in fact extremely high indeed – he was deeply involved with a very well-organised, serious criminal network. It was not as though he could decide one day to pack it in and do something else: he now knew too much. Also, compared with the value of the goods he was transporting and the trouble he would be in if he were caught by the police, he was in fact being paid very little for his services. Having said that, he could hardly go to John Bootle and ask for a pay rise because he now knew what they were smuggling.

Pete had kept in touch with Simon Ashley, the lad he had met and befriended in Strangeways. They would occasionally meet up for a pint and a chat at a pub just behind Piccadilly Gardens after Pete had reported into the office at Wade's on a Friday before travelling back to Anglesey. It was at one of those catchups a couple of weeks after his new discovery that Simon mentioned that Jerry Duggan had just been released from Strangeways. His uncle had asked him to pass on a message to arrange a meeting between the two of them in Manchester.

"When is that happening?" asked Pete without thinking. An idea was quickly forming in his mind and he wanted to have a chat with Jerry to see if he would be interested.

"Why, what's it to you?" Simon replied suspiciously.

"Nothing, mate. I met up with Jerry a few times in the yard after you were released. We got on OK and if he was in town, I'd like to say hello, that's all. When you speak to him, could you give him my number and ask him to call me?"

"OK Pete, I'll pass it on but don't get your hopes up. He's not the social, chatty type and, like I said before, he's also not the sort of guy you want to get involved with."

After that, the conversation drifted back to the usual topics of football, how Man City were doing and reminiscing about when they were kids back at school and on the estate in Wythenshawe.

The following week, to Pete's complete surprise and immense joy, his own personal mobile, one of three he always now carried with him and whose number he had given to Simon, rang while he was driving home to Moelfre after picking up the stock for the following day's trip to Dublin. The number was withheld but he pulled over and answered it, hoping it was Jerry and was relieved when a man with a strong Irish accent asked, "Is that Pete Ainsworth?"

"Yes, is that Jerry?" asked Pete excitedly.

"No, why do you want to speak to him?" the Irish voice replied.

"I have some information which I think might be of interest to him. If we could meet up when he comes to Manchester that would great," continued Pete eagerly.

"I'll let him know. He'll be in touch."

Sure enough, an hour later his phone rang, again from a withheld number and he answered it.

"Pete?" a different Irish voice asked.

"Yes, is that Jerry?"

"What do you want?"

"Can we meet up when you come over to Manchester? I have some business that might be of real interest to you," Pete asked hopefully.

"OK, but don't waste my time son."

"Brilliant, Jerry, I promise you, you won't be disappointed."

"Right, I'll see you at the same pub where you meet Simon, next Friday at about 7pm," Jerry said and hung up.

Pete sat in the van for a couple of minutes wondering if he was doing the right thing. He knew that he was potentially entering very dangerous waters by getting involved with someone like Jerry Duggan but he also knew that if his plan worked then it would at least give him the chance to get out of the mess he had inadvertently got himself in to. After convincing himself that everything would be fine, he started up the engine and continued on his way back home to Moelfre.

Chapter 5

At seven o'clock, as arranged, Pete was nervously sitting in the pub off Piccadilly waiting for Jerry to appear. He had been rehearsing what he was going to say since the call from Jerry; he was hoping this was his big chance to get out of the impossible situation he now found himself in, with a new life and some money in the bank.

Just before 7.30pm, Jerry wandered through from the other bar holding a half empty pint and sat down next to Pete. "OK Pete?" he asked.

"Fine Jerry, thanks for coming. Have you been here for a while, I didn't see you?" Pete replied nervously.

"Finish your drink and we'll go for a ride and a chat," Jerry answered.

They quickly finished their drinks in silence and stood up. Jerry led Pete out of the pub and down Portland Street and into Sackville Street where Jerry got into the back of a silver Audi RS3 which was parked at a meter and pointed to Pete to get into the other rear seat. Without a word, the driver started the car and pulled away from the curb and joined the early evening traffic.

"Right Pete, what have you got?" asked Jerry abruptly.

Pete launched into his well-rehearsed speech with as much confidence as he could muster. "What I need is out. I will give you the opportunity to earn a lot of money and in return, I want a new life, job and identity, preferably in Northern Ireland, and £20,000 in cash. £10,000 initially and then the other £10,000 on completion of the job."

"You don't want much for a small-timer who works as a driver for a clothing company," Jerry sneered.

"I promise you, what I want is small beer compared to your potential earnings and there is almost no risk to you if we plan it right," Pete continued.

"OK you've got my interest, I'm listening."

"Before I give you the details, do you agree to what I want?" he asked with as much bravado as he could muster.

"The new life, job and identity are no problem. I presume someone is going to be very annoyed with what you are proposing?"

"They will be and if they find out it was me who was involved and get hold of me, I would be in very serious trouble indeed. I need to disappear; in fact, it needs to look as though I have been killed so they will eventually give up looking for me."

"You've obviously given this a lot of thought. If the job is worth it, you can have your twenty grand, but I need details."

"I haven't worked it all out, but once a month, usually on a Tuesday night or early Wednesday morning, some goods are delivered to me at my house on Anglesey in a 9x4 inch sealed cylindrical plastic container. Later the same Wednesday morning, I drive into Manchester and pass it in my backpack to the Transport Manager at Wade's where I work in Trafford

Park. He removes the container and replaces it with £1,000 cash for me. I then pick up the bag from his office and drive back to Anglesey where I carry on with my usual trips to Dublin until the next container arrives. So once I receive the container, I need to pass it to you and, with your help, fake some kind of incident where it looks like the bungalow has been ransacked, as though someone was looking for something, there's my blood at the scene, I have totally disappeared but all my things including the van, my wallet, passport and keys are still there. If we do it right, the police will have a mysterious disappearance but with no body or leads to follow up on they will eventually stop looking. Hopefully, my people will presume I have been killed, the cylinder taken and my body buried or perhaps dumped at sea. You provide me with a new ID – passport, driver's licence, credit cards and stuff. I hide out somewhere on the island for a couple of days and then, with my new ID, get the ferry over to Dublin and either you pick me up or I make my way up to Belfast and meet you there. What do you think?"

"What's in the tubes?" Jerry asked bluntly.

"I don't know with 100% certainty but I know where they come from and how they get here, plus someone has gone to a lot of trouble and expense to get them to Anglesey and the people at Wade's have also invested a lot of time and money in bringing them to Trafford Park," Pete cautiously volunteered because he knew this was the one weak link in his plan: he did not know for sure that there were precious stones in the tubes, although he was pretty sure there were. He had to hope it would be too much of a temptation for Jerry to turn down the opportunity. Pete paused for a few seconds then continued. "They come by container ship from Nigeria. The ship anchors in the bay outside Moelfre where I live in a house owned by Wade's, then two guys in a rubber dinghy with an outboard come ashore in the early hours. One of them brings the tube to my bungalow which is a short distance from the shore and then he leaves the package at my back door and returns to the dinghy and the ship. I'm sure the tube must contain a large number of precious gemstones," Pete finished and nervously waited for Jerry's response.

"Is it always the same ship?" asked Jerry.

"Yes, the *MV Caracas*. It's registered in Panama."

"OK Pete, leave it with me. When is the next tube due and how much notice do you get?"

"They are not at any particular interval, usually one a month but always on a Tuesday night/Wednesday morning. The first text is usually about ten days before the delivery which is how long it normally takes the ship to sail from Nigeria to Moelfre and then the follow-up text comes a couple of days before delivery with the confirmed day and date. I suppose that is just in case they hit bad weather on the sail over."

"Right, I'll be in touch. Where do you want dropping?" While they had been talking, they had just been driving round South Manchester at a leisurely speed going nowhere in particular.

"Behind Piccadilly Station would be fine. I've left the van

in a car park there."

The traffic was extremely busy as they headed back into town and it took them forty-five minutes to complete the three-mile journey. They dropped Pete off at his car park and, as they had already completed their business with Simon's uncle, they headed off to Liverpool and the ferry back over to Northern Ireland. Pete found the van and joined the exodus from the city onto Princess Road, Princess Parkway and the M56 to North Wales and home to Anglesey, hoping against hope that Jerry would go for his plan and that he could start a new life somewhere in Northern Ireland, far away from Wade Manufacturing Limited.

It was two long weeks before Jerry finally got back in touch with Pete and it was a simple text to the same private phone: "Same place 7pm next Friday."

As before, Pete was in place a little early but this time it was not Jerry but the driver of the Audi from their last meeting who came through the main door of the pub, nodded at Pete to follow him and went back out. Pete got up, took a quick drink from his half full pint and left the pub. This time the man walked towards the station, went round to the car park they had dropped Pete off at last time, walked through the cars until he came to the same silver Audi, opened the driver's door, signalled Pete to get into the front passenger seat and then got in himself.

"Hi Pete, my name is Mick O'Hare, you remember me from last time?" Pete nodded, taken aback by Jerry's non-appearance and thinking he must not be interested after all.

"Jerry couldn't make it tonight but he is going to go ahead with your plan."

"Brilliant," Pete said with a huge sigh of relief. "What happens next?"

"We will need a bit of time to organise your ID and paperwork. Do you have any particular name in mind?"

"Yes, I thought Paul Andrews, same initials. No particular reason just fancied it but not bothered really."

"OK we'll see what we can do. Once we are ready to go, we will let you know and then as soon as you get the next delivery notification, send a text to this number."

Pete copied the number into his private phone directory.

"I will try and book that cottage further up the lane from Plas Meirion plus another one over near Holyhead, both for two weeks for myself and my wife Aileen. It's off-season now so we have a good chance. If I'm successful, we will go for that delivery, if not we'll keep trying until we get both properties at the same time as the delivery. After the drop, we will come down to you, you give me the cylinder and we will stage the bungalow. We'll use some of your blood, not too much so don't worry, and then we'll drive you over to the other house near Holyhead where you'll stay out of sight for a few days until we think it's OK for you to travel. We'll go back to the cottage near your place and then, in the morning, we'll call 101 and report a bit of a disturbance at Plas Meirion during the night. We'll say we are recently arrived holiday makers and that we are not sure if it was anything serious. We will hang around to answer any questions with the police and occasionally pop over to see you when we think it is OK. Depending on what happens with the police, we'll decide when it is safe for you to leave, and then you get the ferry to Dublin with your new identity and £10,000 in the bank. We will arrange for someone to pick you up from somewhere in Dublin and take you up to Belfast where Jerry will meet you and take it from there."

Everything fell into place beautifully. Mick was able to book both holiday lets in time for the very next delivery and he and Aileen appeared at Plas Meirion fifteen minutes after the drop was made. They went through the house as if they were looking for something, emptying all the drawers, cupboards and wardrobes, and turning over the beds and furniture. They got Pete to cut his left hand, spread some of his blood over one of the chairs and at the front doorway and a bit on the front porch and then bandaged it up. The three of them then drove over to the house at Holyhead, leaving Pete and the cylinder there. Mick and Aileen then returned to Moelfre and, at 9.30 the following morning, Mick dialled 101 to report "a bit of a disturbance" at Plas Meirion and left his name and contact mobile number. The police turned up around midday and briefly interviewed Mick and Aileen before driving down the narrow, winding lane to Plas Meirion. When they got there, they immediately realised that this was more than a minor disturbance – in fact, it had the appearance of a major incident. They immediately called Colwyn Bay and reported it to the Duty Sergeant who told them to make sure no one went in or touched anything and to wait until someone arrived to take over. Fifty minutes later, Detective Sergeant Charlie Watkins arrived, took a quick look round and then went outside to make a call on his mobile. His second call was to Detective Chief Inspector John Wyn Jones. "Afternoon boss, I'm over on Anglesey following a 101 call this morning about some minor disturbance but there looks to be more to it. You don't need to come over, I'll deal with it and fill you in when I get back. See you later." With that, DS Watkins went back into the house, had a quick look round each room, noted the blood and then said to the two constables as he left, "Hang around until forensics get here, don't touch anything and make sure nobody goes in there, OK."

"No problem, Sarge," replied one of the constables.

With that, DS Watkins got back into his car, made another couple of calls on his mobile and drove off back to the mainland.

Pete stayed in the house for another five days, apart from the Saturday when Mick smuggled him out for a couple of hours in the back of his rented Kia SUV while the cleaners came in for their weekly visit. Then, with a new haircut and hair colour and ten days growth of facial hair, Mick dropped him off at the Holyhead Ferry Terminal, complete with a new identity and a one-way ticket to Dublin.

Chapter 6

At 8 o'clock, as arranged, John arrived at their local pub in Moelfre.

"Show me the text," John said as soon as he had bought his drink and joined Steve at their usual table in the corner by the window. Steve got his phone out, found the text and opening it passed the phone to John.

"It's from a with-held number surprise, surprise," Steve volunteered.

"That's a bit melodramatic don't you think Steve? Sounds like someone has been watching too many television dramas to me and they thought it would be funny to try and put the wind up you. I presume you're on Facebook or Twitter or some other social media site so it's easy for people to find your contact details these days."

"Don't you think it's serious then John? When I saw it, my first reaction was more along the lines of 'oh shit'."

"We can't ignore it for sure but I think it's more likely some locals having a bit of a laugh at your expense. There have always been a few of them in the pub when we've been discussing it and I'm sure Andy and Bernie will have been telling others about your interest in the property – they are both well-known local gossips. Let me know if anything else happens out of the ordinary or if you get any more texts and

I'll let Charlie know just in case."

With that, they got back to their normal Tuesday evening socialising, discussing the weather, sport and their various aches and pains.

Later that same evening, John called his old DS, apologised for the lateness of the call and informed him of the new development but Charlie agreed that it was probably a prank by some locals and not anything to worry about. He thanked John for the call and hung up.

At 9.05 the following morning, Sue Greenhalgh, the PA to Brian Mather the Operations Director at Wade Manufacturing Limited, received a call on his private line.

"Good morning, Wade's," Sue answered.

"Hi Sue, it's Tricia at Underwood's, I have Jonathon on the line for Brian," Tricia Scott, the Office Manager at Jonathon T Underwood Solicitors announced.

"Hi Tricia, I'll just see if he is free." Sue put her on hold and called through to Brian's office.

"Brian, I have Jonathon Underwood on the line for you."

"OK Sue, put him through," replied Brian wondering what the hell he wanted first thing in the morning. He did not particularly like the guy, especially the way Jonathon talked to him with his upper-class, condescending manner as though Brian was a bit of a wayward schoolboy. He had been that way with him ever since they first met back in 2001 when he had defended Brian after he got busted for that post office job back in Swansea. But he was also the man who had recruited him for and ran the Nigeria gem smuggling

52

operation so he was a very necessary evil.

Jonathon T Underwood had studied Law (Crime and Criminal Justice), LLB (Hons) at Swansea University; he graduated in July 2001 and joined the team at the newly formed Public Defenders Service office in Swansea in the September where he was involved in the defence of the then 21-year-old Brian Mather in the November. He had worked for the PDS in Swansea for just over eleven years before setting up his own business as a sole practitioner in the centre of Manchester on West Mosely Street in 2013. Jonathon contacted Brian three years after moving to Manchester and was appointed the company lawyer for Wade's, on Brian's recommendation, shortly afterwards. What Brian did not know about him, in fact it was known to very few people, was that Jonathon had adopted his mother's maiden name at the age of sixteen, shortly after his father's untimely death in a swimming pool "accident" at his Marbella villa. Jonathon was actually the only son of Freddie Jones, the leader of a very successful three-man armed robbery gang working out of London and specialising in armoured vans used for transporting large amounts of cash to and from various banks within the City limits.

"Morning, Jonathon."

"Good morning Brian, how the devil are you?" Jonathon asked breezily.

"Fine thanks and you?" replied Brian.

"Absolutely top-hole old chap. Brian, a little birdy tells me you have been sending rather ill-conceived text messages, well one to be specific."

Brian wondered how he knew about that – and so quickly; he had only sent it yesterday. "What text Jonathon?" he asked defensively.

"Come, come old chap, I think we both know to which text I am alluding. Your little missive to our nosey parker in Moelfre."

"Oh that," admitted Brian. "How the hell did you find out about that?"

"I like to know all about what goes on with my various business partners when it potentially affects my own interests, especially in this instance when we are planning to open up our very profitable supply line through North Wales again very shortly. The last thing we want to do is attract any renewed interest in our operations over there. Granted the man's enquiries regarding our little property were certainly an unfortunate coincidence timewise but it was being handled locally. Your text has muddied the waters somewhat, but fortunately it's nothing that cannot be handled. It just means we will monitor the situation for a while longer and, if all is well, simply put the operation back a few weeks. Please leave this to me and I will let you know when the bungalow will be ready for your new man. I presume you have organised the replacement courier I suggested – we do not want another Peter Ainsworth fiasco do we? On that subject, just to let you know, our enquiries into that most unfortunate incident are still ongoing. We really would like to find out where our missing merchandise ended up and how much that boy of yours was involved. I am informed that the police are not pursuing the matter but we certainly are. I think that is all for now Brian, have a good day!" Jonathon closed cheerily.

Four weeks later, on Monday 3rd December, after no new developments at Moelfre, Mat Dawson took up residence at Plas Meirion and shortly afterwards continued what had been Pete Ainsworth's deliveries to Dublin for Wade Manufacturing. Although he was initially vetted and recommended by Jonathon Underwood, he had been recruited by John Bootle, and thoroughly coached by him in all his new duties, both the legitimate and the future illegal ones later in the New Year once his cover had been firmly established.

Chapter 7

That same December, after spotting an advert for the upcoming All Wales Property Auction at Llangefni and looking over the auction catalogue, Steve invited his building contractor friend Tom Clarke down for the sale. There were a couple of properties that they thought were worth a look and, after a quick site visit to both of them, they decided to bid on a three-bedroom bungalow which was situated just outside Trearddur Bay on the northwest coast of the island. The same couple had lived in it for over fifty years; the wife had died seven years ago from cancer and her husband had survived her until earlier that year when he also succumbed to the same terrible disease. The bungalow needed a complete refurbishment: new wiring, a new oil-fired central heating system, new kitchen and bathroom and probably an en-suite for the main bedroom. It was quite a big project but it was only half a mile from the fabulous Trearddur Bay beach and Tom knew it would be an ideal holiday let.

Fortunately, they were successful at the auction although they did have to pay £30,000 above the guide price to secure the sale. There were two other local builders who had obviously also recognised the potential and they pushed up the bidding until it had become too much for them, leaving Tom and Steve as the new owners.

Steve put up 30% of the final hammer price plus commission and was detailed to source some local tradesmen, primarily for the central heating, plumbing and rewiring. Tom's building company would handle the rest. Tom was confident the main structure of the property was sound and fortunately it had had a new roof only a couple of years before, following a bad leak which had caused quite a bit of damage to an area of the timber roof trusses and joists above the main bedroom before it had been discovered. They would start the work in the February of the following year and hopefully be completed in time for the start of the 2019 summer season.

His new project would keep Steve busy, but not too busy to stop him keeping an eye on the comings and goings of the new tenant at Plas Meirion.

PART THREE

Chapter 8

Brian arrived promptly at 8.55am for his 9am appointment at West Mosely Street. They had been meeting on the first Monday of each month since, on Brian's recommendation to his wife and newly appointed Managing Director of Wade Manufacturing Limited, the firm of Jonathon T Underwood LLB had been appointed as the company solicitors. At the time, Wade's was struggling to survive and the Managing Director, William Harrison Wade, who was the third generation of the Wade family to own and run the business, had finally retired from his full-time role and become a non-executive director, passing the ailing firm on to his only daughter Joanna. The high-quality leather products they manufactured and sold direct through their shop in Manchester were outdated, expensive and no longer in demand. His daughter was young, ambitious and full of new ideas on how to make Wade's a successful, thriving concern again.

Joanna Wade had had a very successful private education and, in 2002, went to the University of Derby where she gained a first-class honours degree in Textile Design which was followed by a two-year master's degree in Business

Studies at the University of Manchester. She joined her father's firm in 2009 as their new product designer. She met Brian whilst on holiday with a couple of her girlfriends in Marbella in 2011 and married him the following year, very much against her mother and father's wishes. She knew very little about Brian's very chequered history and was not particularly interested. It was a typical whirlwind holiday romance and she was madly in love with him from the moment they met in a bar overlooking the marina.

A few years later, shortly after her father semi-retired and she was promoted to Managing Director, Brian had introduced her to Jonathon T Underwood, a Manchester solicitor who Brian said was representing a client who wished to invest in their business. She completely trusted her husband, did not ask too many questions and readily agreed to it as they desperately needed the money. Her father tried to caution her against dealing with an unknown investor but Joanna over-ruled him and they went ahead. Joanna retained fifty-one percent of the company shares and control of the business and all product development and Brian was promoted to Operations Director. An initial five million pounds in the first year, followed by a further five million in both years two and three of their agreement, bought the offshore investment company forty-nine percent of Wade Manufacturing Limited. With the money, Joanna launched her new range of up-market leisurewear and, on Brian's suggestion, opened two new retail outlets in London and Dublin. The company had gone from strength to strength.

At nine o'clock, Brian was shown through to Jonathon's office by Tricia Scott who knocked on the door, opened it and showed him in.

"Morning Brian, I trust you are well," Jonathon greeted him warmly.

"Very well thanks, Jonathon," Brian replied eagerly, keen to start the meeting which he hoped would herald the start of their gemstone smuggling operation again.

"Excellent old chap. Joanna has sent over the figures for the last six months' sales, very satisfactory," continued the solicitor who was purposely stalling Brian from discussing the main topic of the visit just for the fun of it. "I have forwarded them to our partners who I am pleased to say are very happy with the company's performance." Brian nodded, anxious to move on to the real reason for their meeting.

"When can we start the deliveries again Jonathon? Mat Dawson has settled in at Moelfre and been delivering regularly again to Dublin. He's sure nobody is taking any interest in him and is ready to go."

Jonathon smiled to himself, paused for a few seconds and then finally conceded. "Yes, it would appear that everything has returned to normal down there. Your ill-judged text message to Mr Guest fortunately has not had any serious repercussions and I understand he has now switched his attentions to a project on the other side of the island at Trearddur Bay which is very reassuring. I agree with you and I think we can resume deliveries as before. I will contact our representatives in Nigeria and place an order for the merchandise to be delivered monthly as before. I see no reason to change any of the details of our previous arrangements. One other thing Brian. As I mentioned, our overseas investors are very happy with the company's performance over the last couple of years and feel that it would be a good time to look at a further expansion. Especially impressive is the increase in the online sales figures for the last twelve months, something which I know has been a pet project of your wife's and I know she has pushed the idea of expanding that side of the business recently. I am pleased to tell you that the investors agree and I will be putting forward, in conjunction with our accountants, a firm proposal at our upcoming annual board meeting next month. If you could ask Joanna to put together a set of plans outlining her expansion proposals, we could discuss them at length and agree how we might move forward." Jonathon paused and looked at Brian.

Emrys Williams, the sole partner of Williams & Co, was, in addition to being Underwood's and Wade's official accountants, the silent partner in all Jonathon's illicit activities. Emrys had been employed at a large accountancy firm in Cardiff when the two senior partners were successfully prosecuted and convicted of various money laundering, embezzlement and fraud charges. Emrys was not found to be directly or knowingly involved in any illegal activities, although he was involved, unwittingly according to his solicitor, in many of the international money transfers to the various offshore accounts that the two criminal accountants were using.

Jonathon himself was not involved in the prosecution case but he had noted Emrys's part in the operations and filed it away for future reference. Eighteen months after the trial had concluded and the dust had settled, Jonathon had made contact with the newly qualified articled accountant on the pretext of his interest in Emrys's ex-employer's prosecution to assess if Emrys would perhaps be open to joining him in his future ventures both legal and perhaps even illegal, thus making use of his knowledge of offshore banking transactions. After building an initial mutual trust, it soon became apparent to Jonathon that Emrys had not been completely innocent and, although he was not directly involved in the illegal activities, he eventually admitted to the solicitor that he had been aware of what had been going on; he also admitted he was not unduly concerned by the illegal activity, his only regret appeared to be that they had been caught, prosecuted and ended up in prison. In fact, after one particularly long lunch involving the consumption of a couple of bottles of particularly fine red wine, he hinted to Jonathon that he had, unbeknownst to his previous employers and the crown prosecution, diverted some of the money from one of the offshore accounts into another one that he had set up for himself shortly before their offices were raided and the two senior partners charged. The following year, Jonathon moved to Manchester and Emrys set up his new accountancy firm in Swansea and their mutually beneficial partnership was sealed.

Jonathon knew that his and Emrys's proposal would be warmly welcomed by Joanna and would be voted through at the board meeting.

"That would be brilliant Jonathon, Joanna will be really pleased," Brian beamed.

"If there is nothing else, I think that concludes our business for today Brian. Once everything is in place with Nigeria, I will be in touch. As our ex-colonial cousins would say, 'have a good day!'"

With that, Brian stood up and, after saying cheerio to Tricia, left the office. He still could not believe how his life had turned around since the chance meeting with Joanna Wade in that bar in Marbella. He had been born and brought up on a council estate in Swansea. After a misspent youth and little formal education, he had followed his father into a life of petty crime until he had got involved as the driver with a small-time team of thieves who specialised in robbing village post offices and more remote petrol stations throughout South Wales. They were finally and inevitably caught and went to trial in Swansea in November 2001; the main gang members received getting short custodial sentences as no one was ever injured in the robberies and Brian, as the driver, was given a suspended sentence with community service. He was defended by a young solicitor from the newly formed Public Defenders Service in Swansea which is where he first met Jonathon T Underwood LLB who was to play such a major role in his later life. Then fifteen years later, shortly after Joanna had been made Managing Director at Wade's and completely out of the blue, Jonathon had contacted him and outlined the investment offer. He had stressed to Brian that the offer was conditional on him being appointed as their company solicitor and Williams & Co of Swansea being engaged as their new accountancy firm and financial consultants; he had also suggested to Brian, off the record, that if they went ahead, there would be various lucrative opportunities available to him personally at a later date. Joanna had readily agreed despite her father's reticence and their company and his private income had grown steadily in value ever since. What Brian did not know was that there was, in fact, no overseas investment company – the money was part of Jonathon's private illegal fortune which was being "washed" through the company, one of a number of similar arrangements he had in place, some with other former clients from his Public Defenders Service days in Swansea. These included several private companies around the country, a jewellery wholesaler and retail business in Manchester, a fine art gallery in London and his newly acquired auction business just off the M6 north of Birmingham which specialised in high-value cars both modern and vintage, fine art and antiques and, not surprisingly, high-value customised jewellery.

Brian returned to his office in Trafford Park and called his Transport Manager. "We are on again John, give Mat a call and make sure he knows exactly what to do when he gets the go-ahead. Run through everything with him when he is next in the office. Hopefully we should get the first delivery pretty soon now."

"Great news Brian, leave it to me," replied his colleague.

Across in Manchester, Jonathon Underwood was also

making a call regarding the Nigerian merchandise – not the upcoming shipment, but the one that had gone astray after being delivered to Peter Ainsworth. He had finally received a tip-off from one of the illegal dealers he knew who had heard about some gemstones similar to the missing ones which had surfaced in Northern Ireland. He called the dealer who gave him a number to call which was a PAYG mobile. When he rang it, someone with a strong Irish accent answered and, after Jonathon gave a prearranged code name, he was told that the man who had sold the stones to a fellow dealer was called Jerry Duggan before the man immediately rang off. 'At last,' Jonathon thought, 'we have something to work with.' He took out one of the PAYG mobiles from the top drawer of his desk and dialled the only number in the directory. "I finally have a name which could be connected to the loss of our merchandise. He is called Jerry Duggan and is probably based in Belfast. Find out what you can and get back to me." With that, he ended the call.

The same phone rang in less than an hour.

"That was quick, what have you got?" asked Jonathon.

"I think you have your man or one of them at least. He didn't take much finding, he has a file a couple of inches thick. He was in Strangeways at the same time as our young mister Ainsworth, which is where they must have met, although I don't know how because they would have moved in completely different circles. Duggan was doing a stretch for armed robbery and is a serious criminal and has no connection to Ainsworth other than being at Strangeways at the same time but it's too much of a coincidence not to tie him to it. I don't have anything on Duggan after he was released, he seems to have kept a low profile. I'll keep digging and see if I can turn anything else up. Something you do need to know if you intend trying to find this guy is that he keeps very bad company. One of his main associates according to my source is a certain Michael O'Hare who apparently is one very nasty piece of work. Duggan is very high up in the Belfast underworld, nothing to do with the paramilitaries, just an out and out villain but he would be hard to get at over there."

"Excellent, thanks for that. You keep on digging and see if you can come up with an address for our Mr Duggan although from what you say, we may have to try and arrange some kind of meeting with him if and when he comes across the water, and sooner rather than later. It would appear that we can certainly say goodbye to our property, but some form of retribution is certainly in order if at all possible – we can't have criminals stealing from us now can we? Plus, he could pose a threat if he gets wind of our renewed activities, he might want a second piece of our cake. No, Mr Duggan needs neutralising one way or another."

Jonathon ended the call, took out another of his PAYG phones and dialled a new number.

Chapter 9

The following day, Steve Guest received a text from John Wyn Thomas asking if he was free to meet that evening at their local pub for a chat and catch up. Steve had not seen John since before Christmas so he was intrigued by the invitation, especially as he had definitely got the impression that John's interest in the Peter Ainsworth disappearance had waned when they were last together.

Steve arrived just before eight o'clock to find John already sat at his usual table by the window with an almost empty pint.

"Evening John," Steve greeted him, "been here a while? Want another?"

"Yes and yes please," replied John with a smile.

Steve ordered two pints and took them over to the table and sat down opposite John. "To what do I owe this pleasure?" Steve asked. "Not seen you for a while, had a good Christmas?"

"I thought we should meet for a catch up and no, not particularly, I always find it a particularly boring time. I have no close family and I come from the "Bah Humbug" school of Christmas celebrants."

"Sorry I asked," Steve smiled.

"How is your building renovation going over at Trearddur,

have you started yet?" John asked.

"It's early days, Tom my builder friend has done the initial investigations and started ripping out all the old fittings and so far no problems. I've engaged a local electrician and central heating installation firm so it all seems to be going to plan. Tom reckons we should be ready for the holiday letting season by Easter."

After the usual pleasantries had been exchanged involving their general health, the weather and the dire state of the country and the various political parties, John brought the conversation round to the main reason for the meeting. He surprised Steve by confirming that he was, in fact, still very much interested in looking into the "Plas Meirion mystery".

"Following our last meeting," John started, "after a lot of thought, I have come to the conclusion that the whole incident and the lack of progress on what happened just does not add up. At the time, as I said, I was coming up to retirement and just did not give it the attention it probably deserved – I thought it was just a simple missing person and left it to my sergeant, presuming it would be sorted pretty quickly. When the investigation appeared to go nowhere and nobody seemed particularly bothered about this lad's disappearance, his family or his employers, and the enquiries into the company and the solicitor turned up nothing of interest, it just ended up on the "ongoing investigation" pile. I retired and, as far as I could see, it was all forgotten about. Then by accident you got interested in the case and shortly afterwards you received that strange text which we all dismissed as a joke based on our previous assumptions that the affair was a simple unexplained missing persons case. But then I thought, what if there was more to it and the disappearance wasn't the main point of the incident and the text was in fact a genuine threat?"

John paused and Steve broke in. "So you think there is more to it then?" he asked excitedly. "That's brilliant, what do you suggest we do?"

"I've been doing quite a bit of digging of my own already over the last couple of months – it's amazing what you can find out nowadays if you know where to look. Using public records, social media and some of my contacts in the force, the ones I knew I could trust, I have uncovered some very interesting facts and that's why I suggested we meet. Have you been doing any investigating on your own recently?" John asked seriously.

"Well yes, the building conversion doesn't take up much of my time so I have been trying to keep an eye on the new tenant at Plas Meirion, his comings and goings. It seems strange that Wade's have kept that particular bungalow for their delivery man to Dublin after the last guy's disappearance. Why would they do that when he could be based anywhere? I don't understand why the police haven't looked into that more."

"Have you turned up anything about the new guy?" John asked.

"No, absolutely nothing. As far as I can see he just travels between Moelfre, Manchester and Dublin twice a week, always around the same times, and keeps very much to himself. I have spent several nights watching the end of his road, being careful not to be noticed of course, and I have never seen him leaving or returning during the night. I even rented the bungalow up from his for a week over New Year and didn't see anything untoward and I never left the place. As I said, I've been very careful and I'm pretty sure he doesn't suspect I have been watching him. What have you found out, anything interesting?"

"Yes, and that's why I called you. I think something serious has been going on here in the past and, because there is a new tenant at Plas Meirion, I think it has started again or is about to. You need to back off until I find out exactly what it is and who is involved," John explained. "Same again?" he asked as he stood up and started towards the bar.

John came back to the table with the two pints and Steve sat expectantly, waiting for him to continue. "I won't go over everything I have discovered so far but I can tell you that I firmly believe that Peter Ainsworth's disappearance from Plas Meirion is not a simple missing persons case. Like you, the more I thought about it the more I was convinced that the investigation was all a bit superficial. As it was almost entirely carried out by DS Watkins, that was the first thing that attracted my attention so I did a bit of checking. He joined us from Manchester less than a year before this all happened and I must admit I didn't know a lot about him. I seem to remember his move was something to do with his mother-in-law moving into a care home at Menai Bridge and his wife

70

wanting to be near to her. He was a good sergeant and I certainly didn't have any problems with him but I thought I would do a bit of a background check anyway just to be thorough. I spoke to an ex-colleague of mine from Colwyn Bay who is a good personal friend and he put me in touch with a guy who works in admin at Charlie's old station at Newton Heath in Manchester. I gave him a story about arranging a bit of an anniversary get-together for Charlie, saying I just wanted a bit of background about his service there and to keep it quiet as it was going to be a surprise do. He was a bit reticent about giving me anything specific but did confirm amongst a few other general bits of information that he had only been at Manchester for a few years and had originally come from South Wales, Swansea to be precise.

"At first, nothing struck a chord or seemed out of place – he was well thought of and did a good, if not spectacular job. But then when I started looking at Wade's and their solicitor, something I should have done during the original investigation, a very strange coincidence appeared. Jonathon Underwood went to Swansea University and worked for the Public Defenders Service in Swansea for many years before setting up his private practice in Manchester. The final pieces of the puzzle fell into place when I found out that Brian Mather, the Operations Director at Wade's, also came from Swansea originally and he was defended by Jonathon Underwood while he was at the PDS – Mather was the driver on a post office job down there. Not only are Wade's accountants also based in Swansea, but the head of that firm,

Emrys Williams, previously worked for a firm which was prosecuted in a big money laundering and fraud case in Cardiff, although he was not found to be directly involved at the time. Put that all together and you get the potential for a serious conspiracy. Until I get some idea what is going on at Wade's and Moelfre I want you to stop whatever it is you are doing with regards to this – we could be dealing with some very serious criminal activity and we don't want what happened to Peter Ainsworth happening to you."

"Okay John, I hear you. What do you propose we do?" asked Steve nervously; his original light-hearted detective hobby had taken on a new, extremely serious aspect and he knew he was very much out of his depth. He was very grateful that it was the ex-Detective Chief Inspector who was his accomplice and confidant and he felt all the safer for it.

"As I said, you do nothing. We are looking at the possibility that a well-respected solicitor and accountant and a current serving senior police officer are involved in some serious crime – not something to casually bandy about in conversation, especially if it is true. If they are, we don't know who else may be involved and who we can trust. All we have at the moment are a series of questions. Yes, we know that the three men are potentially linked and something probably happened at Moelfre other than a simple 'missing person' but at the moment, that is all we know for sure. What we don't know is who is involved, what they are doing, if they are still doing it and what really happened to Peter Ainsworth. Has he just gone walk-about or is he floating out in the Irish Sea or buried somewhere in the Anglesey countryside? I think that the key to all of this is Underwood the solicitor – whatever is going on or has gone on is very likely to be under his control. Mather is small-time and I think Underwood is just using him. I have done quite a bit of research on Wade's and, as a company, it definitely comes up clean. I think Mather is working independently for Underwood and is using his delivery man at Moelfre as some kind of go-between, like Peter Ainsworth before him, in addition to his legitimate duties for the company. What for, however, I have no idea yet."

"It has got to be something to do with the house at Moelfre surely," interrupted Steve eagerly, "otherwise, why would they continue to use it? It can't be just because it is convenient for the ferries to Dublin because any property on Anglesey would fit that bill. It must be something to do with that particular location at Moelfre."

"It would seem so, I agree," answered the retired Detective Chief Inspector, "but you said that you've been watching the property for the last couple of months and not seen anything in the least bit suspicious, just a delivery man going about his business."

"True," conceded Steve, "but perhaps they've not started doing again whatever it is they did with Peter before he disappeared."

With that, they both fell silent and looked out of the window at the fabulous view over the bay to Puffin Island, Snowdonia and the Great Orme at Llandudno in the distance. They finished their drinks in silence and then with a promise by Steve to leave well alone and by both of them to keep in touch they got up and left the pub together.

When Steve arrived back home, he mulled over what John had told him and decided that he would do as he was instructed up to a point, but he determined to keep a wary eye on Plas Meirion from a safe distance whenever possible. He did not want to leave all the investigating to the ex-policeman.

Three weeks later, he had still not seen anything out of the ordinary at Moelfre and he had not heard back from John.

Chapter 10

The annual general meeting of Wade Manufacturing Limited was held in the boardroom at their Trafford Park main office. Attending were Joanna Mather (Managing Director), Brian Mather (Operations Director), William H Wade (Non-Executive Director), Jonathan T Underwood (Company Solicitor), Emrys Williams (Senior Partner of Williams & Co, the company's accountants) and Sue Greenhalgh (PA to Brian and acting Company Secretary) and it was opened promptly at 11am by Jonathan.

"Good morning all and welcome. Sue has kindly previously circulated the Annual Report for your perusal, professionally produced as ever by Emrys's firm and I am sure you will all agree it makes excellent reading. Has anyone got any comments or queries they would like to raise?" Jonathon looked expectantly around the room and when no one answered he continued. "In that case, if no one has any questions, can we proceed to the main subject of today's meeting, item one on the agenda, the proposal to open a new online sales division within Wade's. We have identified a vacant warehouse with an enclosed office area close by on Trafford Park which would be perfect for us and Emrys has put together a detailed finance plan which I hope you have all received?" Again Jonathon looked around the table to confirm that everyone was nodding in acknowledgement. "The financials cover the purchase of the land and buildings, the projected additional staff and equipment requirements for both the office and the warehouse, based on consultations with Joanna and with Brian about the additional transportation and home delivery needs. On the transport side, we have proposed that we initially subcontract that to a Liverpool company that Emrys and I know well and have used before, McConnell Transport and Warehousing, until we can further assess exactly what our requirements will be before we invest in any additional company vehicles and drivers. This is a major expansion for the company but both our investment partners and Emrys believe, following the excellent sales figures over the last two years and Joanna's projections, that it is a very prudent and cost effective one. Any comments?"

William was the first to speak.

"It is a very impressive plan Jonathon and so are the projected costs. I know you represent the investors who you insist wish to preserve their anonymity, but I must admit to a certain degree of nervousness and reticence in agreeing to such a large investment from someone we know nothing about."

"We have had this conversation before William. I understand your reservations but as I explained when we first met and I presented the initial investment package, which you must agree has proved profitable for all parties, this is how they operate. Emrys has dealt with this company on many similar investment packages with various companies and they have always delivered on their promises," Jonathon patiently explained.

"Exactly William," Brian joined in. "We knew what we were getting into and it has proven a great success. Their investment not only saved the company but under Joanna's direction, and with your help and guidance of course, it has gone from strength to strength."

"That's the point Brian," William replied, "we don't know what and who we are dealing with."

"You are dealing with a company that I represent and that is bona fide, I absolutely guarantee it William," Jonathon continued smoothly. "Surely that is sufficient?"

"Yes Dad, I agree with Brian and Jonathon and I'm happy to go ahead with the expansion."

"Fine, it's your company now Joanna but I would like my reservations minuted," William conceded.

Emrys spoke for the first time.

"As Jonathon said, I deal with this investment house regularly on behalf of several companies and have done so for many years. As you all know, it is based on Grand Cayman for the obvious tax advantages that all the companies based there enjoy and it has traded successfully for many years and without the slightest hint of any impropriety in all that time, which I presume is your concern William."

After a long silence, during which all the board members looked at the lengthy proposal files, Jonathon finally continued. "Alright then, can we please vote on the proposed expansion plan?" he asked after confirming that they had all completed their scrutiny of the documents.

There was a show of hands and the vote was carried four for, no one against but with one abstention and a quizzical look from William to Jonathon.

The meeting lasted for a further ninety minutes whilst they discussed the expansion project in more detail and was then brought to a close by Jonathon before the five board members adjourned to a favourite restaurant in Manchester's city centre for a long celebratory late lunch.

Chapter 11

When Mathew Dawson arrived as usual on Monday morning at Wade's warehouse in Trafford Park to pick up his first load of stock for the week for their Dublin shop he was met by John Bootle, the Transport Manager.

"Morning Mat, everything alright?"

"Yes thanks Mr Bootle," answered Mathew.

"When you've loaded up, could you pop up to the office for a minute?" the Transport Manager asked.

"Sure no problem, I'll be about forty-five minutes if that's okay," Mathew replied.

Fifty minutes later, Mathew knocked on John Bootle's office door and he was called in.

"Good news Mat, we are good to go with the extra deliveries from Moelfre. You know what to do, we've been through it enough times."

"Great Mr Bootle. Yes, I'll get an initial text on the Nokia phone and then a follow-up one a few days later confirming the day and date of the delivery. I'll get a ring on the back doorbell sometime between 12am and 6am on the morning of the delivery and the cylinder will be left on the doorstep. Five minutes later I go out and get it and then bring it in to you later that same day when I come in for my usual Dublin stock delivery," Mat replied, confirming the delivery arrangements.

"Good lad. You bring it to me in the office in your backpack and I'll swap it for an envelope with £1,000 cash for you. If everything goes well, we should get around one a month, not a bad bonus for you," John said with a big smile on his face.

"That everything Mr Bootle?" Mathew asked as he rose to leave.

"Yes, have a good week Mat and drive safely. Don't forget to let me know when you get the texts."

"Will do." With that, Mathew left the office, went down to the warehouse, picked up his fully stocked Transit and set off back to Moelfre ready for the early morning ferry to Dublin the next day.

As soon as Mathew left, the Transport Manager went across to Brian Mather's office in the main administration block. When she saw him, Brian's PA, Sue Greenhalgh, called through on the intercom, "John Bootle is here to see you Brian."

"Okay Sue, send him through."

Sue nodded at John and he went into Brian's office.

"Just been through everything with Mat, should be fine Brian."

"Better had be John, we won't get another chance if anything goes wrong again. I' sure I don't have to tell you to keep a close eye on Mathew – we don't want another fiasco like we had with Pete Ainsworth do we?" Brian said pointedly.

The Transport Manager winced and looked at the floor. He had been instrumental in hiring Pete through one of his former contacts, current employee Harry Grimes, who was another of his "special" drivers. John knew that both he and Harry had been lucky to come through that episode unscathed – the loss of the gemstones was a serious blow to their little consortium and they were pretty sure that Pete had been involved in some way.

"Let me know when the next delivery is due John."

"Will do Brian," and with that the Transport Manager turned and left the office.

"Sue, could you get me Jonathon Underwood please," Brian asked his PA on the intercom after John had left.

"Straight away Brian," Sue replied as she dialled Jonathon Underwood's private line. It was answered almost immediately and Brian was put through.

"Morning Brian old chap, how the devil are you?" Jonathon asked cheerily.

"Fine thanks Jonathon. Just a quick call to let you know we are all good at our end. When can we expect the first delivery?"

"Very soon I should think. I have confirmed our order with my contact and he assures me everything is in place again. Let me know when we have a date won't you? Sorry to be abrupt but I am just in the middle of something. Cheerio." With that, Jonathon rang off.

Sure enough, two weeks later Mathew Dawson received the first text on his company Nokia PAYG phone announcing the imminent arrival of his first "special delivery". It duly arrived on his back doorstep at 3.15am the following Wednesday. As arranged, he delivered the package to his Transport Manager in his new red backpack later that same day, who then swapped it for a slim brown envelope containing £1,000 in used £20 notes. They were back in the gemstone smuggling business.

Chapter 12

It was some time after their last meeting that Steve received the eagerly awaited text from John Wyn Thomas inviting him to meet again that Tuesday evening. As before, John was already sat by the window but this time with an almost full pint of his favourite tipple. Steve bought himself a pint of lager and joined him at the table.

"Evening John," Steve said happily. John nodded and took a drink from his glass. "Everything good?" he asked.

"Yes, fine thanks," the retired policeman replied.

"I presume you have some news?" Steve asked.

"Yes and no," replied John thoughtfully. "I have a lot more information concerning our solicitor chap and his accountant but I am no closer to understanding what is going on except that I am now completely convinced that something seriously illegal is happening, and not just at Moelfre with Wade's."

"What have you learnt John?" Steve asked expectantly.

"As I said before, I'm convinced it all centres round this solicitor Underwood but we have to be very careful that he doesn't get wind that either you or I are still interested in him or Wade's. It was pure luck we are looking into it because if they had closed down the Moelfre operation and moved it somewhere else the enquiry would have remained dormant and he would be doing whatever it is completely in the clear. Anyway, as I said, I didn't want to chance being caught looking into his affairs in case my former colleague DS Watkins is involved, and I'm pretty sure he is by the way.

"So a couple of weeks ago I contacted a private investigator I know and asked him as a favour to see what he could find out about our Mr Underwood. I had put some business his way when I was in the force and he readily agreed. I met up with him yesterday and he told me what he had found out so far. There is nothing obviously illegal as far as he can see, either with the work Underwood is doing or the companies he represents, but there are some very interesting coincidences. As you found out when you innocently contacted his offices, he is not in general practice, he seems to only work for a few retained clients. So far, the investigator has found that there are at least six companies he officially represents including Wade's and they all appear to be perfectly legitimate but he thinks there might be other businesses he is involved with as well. The names of these six are irrelevant but there are some similarities when you look at them closely. You like a puzzle Steve, don't you? These are the other five company addresses: Bede Trading Estate, Jarrow; Dairycoates Industrial Estate, Hull; Nuffield Industrial Estate, Poole; Waterloo Industrial Estate, Pembroke; Grain Industrial Estate, Liverpool. What strikes you about them, forgetting Wade's for the moment? Apart from the obvious – that they are all on industrial estates, although that does allow for lots of traffic at all times of the day and night without arousing any suspicion."

Steve thought about it for a minute then replied, "My geography isn't great, but aren't they all near the coast?"

"Yes, you're almost there. The really interesting thing is that they are all near ports and ports which have direct connections via ferries to other parts of Europe. Jarrow, which is just outside Newcastle, to Amsterdam, Hull to Zeebrugge and Rotterdam, Poole to Cherbourg, Pembroke to Rosslare and of course Liverpool to a couple of destinations in Northern Ireland. The second coincidence is that all six of them, including Wade's, changed their accountants to a firm based in Swansea shortly after Underwood was appointed their new solicitor. And finally, all six were struggling before he joined them and they all received a large investment via the same offshore investment company through the Swansea accountants as part of their new agreement which the solicitor appears to have brokered. According to my man, everything appears legal and above board if you look at each deal individually, but when looked at overall, and he agrees, it definitely looks very fishy, forgive the pun. Another coincidence is that all the firms have delivery vehicles of some description or other."

"Well Wade's fits in with the deliveries and the ferries if you add in Holyhead, so do you think it is to do with some sort of international delivery network, smuggling, that sort of thing?" Steve asked.

"That is the problem – the companies all seem legitimate and, as I said, their business seems completely above board.

My man also uncovered some very interesting background on the accountant, Emrys Williams, who appears to be involved in most if not all of Underwood's businesses. He originally worked at a large accountancy firm in Cardiff after graduating from the University of South Wales with a first in Accounting and Finance. The firm was involved in a big scandal back in the nineties. The two senior partners were convicted of some pretty serious stuff involving money laundering through offshore companies, embezzlement and a few other serious charges. Emrys was never shown to be involved or charged with anything and soon got a job at another local firm where he completed his accountancy qualifications. Underwood was not directly involved in any of the litigation but it was a big deal at the time in South Wales. Williams set up his own firm shortly before Underwood moved to Manchester – bit of a coincidence don't you think? My man is going to carry on digging but Underwood and Williams are obviously doing a very good job of hiding whatever it is they are involved in and who knows what other pies they have their fingers in which we don't know about and who else might be involved. If what we think is correct, it also means he would not have been stupid enough to send you that threatening text. That must have come from someone else involved in the Plas Meirion affair and I think that is where we should concentrate our activities. I think that might be his weak point – he is too confident or too complacent to change whatever is going on at Moelfre. We know that it involves Plas Meirion and that delivery man, so that should be our target. We'll draw up a rota and between us we'll keep a very close eye on things over there."

They spent the next hour discussing their best plan of action. They knew they would have to be very careful that they did not attract any attention or appear to be acting suspiciously in any way, either to the tenant living at Plas Meirion or indeed to the locals who might report them to the police which would completely blow their plans.

They finally agreed that the driver would probably be adopting whatever routine Peter Ainsworth had used before him and as he had disappeared between Tuesday night and Wednesday morning they decided they would watch the house from Tuesday afternoon through to Wednesday afternoon, split into alternate eight-hour shifts. They would change their positions regularly and decide on them after they had reconnoitred the area around the bungalow when they knew the delivery man was not about.

They had no trouble finding several good vantage points on a couple of nearby abandoned farms and their disused tracks which walkers often used to park their cars before setting off to explore the surrounding countryside and renowned coastal path. From the various places and in the comfort of their cars they could keep watch on the end of the lane which led down to Plas Meirion where it joined the main Moelfre to Amlwch road without arousing any suspicions.

They started their rota the following Tuesday and four weeks later, after observing nothing out of the ordinary with the Wade's delivery man, they started to doubt their theories and to wonder if perhaps there was in fact nothing illegal going on at Moelfre and that it was all just a series of coincidences after all. Steve's wife Carla was also starting to wonder about her husband's sudden interest in mid-week night fishing with his new pal from the pub and, after she had questioned him a couple of times, Steve thought it would be a good idea to have a break from his weekly night excursions.

Steve and John agreed to meet up at the pub to review their strategy and try and decide if they were in fact wasting their time with something that they had got completely wrong.

So five weeks after they started their fruitless investigation, they met up at the pub, arriving together. After buying their drinks, they settled down at a different table at the rear of the pub – it was quieter there and also a couple had already claimed their usual place by the window.

John was the first to speak after a short pause while they both collected their thoughts. "I've been giving this a lot of thought as I'm sure have you." Steve nodded in silent agreement. "Although we have found nothing out of the ordinary so far, I am convinced that there was and is something illegal going on between Brian Mather and this solicitor, there are just too many coincidences and connections between them. But I also think we have been side-tracked by all the information regarding Underwood and his various companies. We presumed they were all linked operationally as well as financially but perhaps they aren't. Perhaps they are only connected in that he uses each company simply for commercial purposes, for money laundering or perhaps even legitimate investments. I still think that the key is here in Moelfre at Plas Meirion. We both agree that there has to be a very good reason why Wade's have kept the bungalow and placed a new delivery man there. I think we have been looking at this from the wrong angle. What we have to discover is what is so special about this particular bungalow. We have been watching the road, thinking it was to do with clandestine deliveries linked to a transport network with the other companies and their potential links to the continent via the various ferry services. But if we take the other companies out of the equation for the moment and just look at Wade's, what is particular about, or specific to, Plas Meirion?"

Steve thought about that and replied slowly, "It's convenient for the ferries to Dublin and it's secluded for anyone wanting to remain anonymous."

"Yes, but so are a host of other houses in the area," replied John. "What is particular to this specific bungalow?"

"It overlooks the bay and is close to the sea?" answered Steve tentatively.

"Exactly Steve – that is precisely what I think we have been missing from the start. Perhaps it is not what goes *out* from Plas Meirion, although I think that eventually something probably does go out. It is the perfect place to have something secretly delivered *to* – and not from the road, from the sea." John paused and looked at Steve, who slowly started to nod in agreement as this new theory slowly sunk in.

"So what do you suggest?" asked Steve with growing

interest and excitement.

"I think we need to move our surveillance from the front of the bungalow to the back where it leads down to the sea. But we will have to be very careful because if something is coming in that way, we have no idea from where or which direction so we will have to be a reasonable distance away and well hidden. I have a few ideas of how we can go about this and also some equipment that we will need." With that, John brought out a notebook and over the next hour outlined his proposals and what they would need for their new surveillance plans.

Chapter 13

Jonathon had not long returned to the office from an extended lunch at one of his favourite Chinese restaurants in Manchester's China Town with his wife Abigail who was on one of her weekly shopping trips when she called his private iPhone. "Yes my dear, what is it?" Jonathon asked wearily.

"Sorry for bothering you darling but I forgot to mention that I'm out this evening with Sandra at Pilates and then we're going on to The Mere with Carol and Fiona to finalise everything for the charity gala dinner on Saturday. Would you mind awfully getting yourself something to eat on the way home tonight as I won't be back until quite late?"

"No problem Abi, have a pleasant evening." Jonathon ended the call and smiled to himself. He had met Abigail at a similar British Heart Foundation charity event at Mere Golf Resort & Spa several years ago, two years after setting up his practice in Manchester. She was ten years younger than him, one of half a dozen models who had been hired by the organisers to meet and greet at the event and he married her a year later. Based at their large, modern five-bedroom house in Wilmslow, she was now a full-time housewife, shopper and very much a member of the very wealthy and illustrious "Cheshire Set". He knew that some of his friends and professional colleagues thought of her as something of a "trophy" bride, someone who looked great by his side at dinners and official functions, but Jonathon truly loved her for herself. Yes, she looked amazing but she was also great fun to be with, always made a fuss of him and best of all made him very happy.

"Tricia, please could you get me Declan or Jimmy at McConnell's?" Jonathon asked his secretary on the intercom after ending the call with his wife.

"Certainly Mr Underwood," Tricia replied as she dialled their private number.

Declan and Jimmy McConnell were twins and Joint Managing Directors of McConnell Transport & Warehousing Limited based in Liverpool. One of the companies directly set up by Jonathon, anonymously through his Swansea accountancy partners, to help service his original criminal activity, it provided a distribution network for his first company investment, Boston Heating & Ventilation Supplies Limited which was based in Hull and whose unofficial business was the importation and distribution of a large amount of Class A drugs. Jonathon had originally met Peter Boston through the PDS in Swansea when he defended, as he was later to find out, one of Boston's dealers who was arrested in Swansea for the sale and supply of drugs. A few years later, Jonathon bought into their business and, through the contacts he had made whilst at the PDS and his new transport company, helped grow it into a multi-million-pound enterprise. The McConnells knew nothing about Jonathon's other line of business originating in Nigeria – he liked to keep the drugs and the gemstones businesses completely separate in every respect; only his partner at the accountants in Swansea knew of both operations.

"I have Declan McConnell for you, Mr Underwood," his secretary announced and put him through.

"Afternoon Declan, I trust you are well?" asked Jonathon.

"Fine thanks Jonathon. What can I do for you?" answered Declan.

"Just a quick call to see if you have made any progress with our Irish friend. Have you heard anything?"

"Hang on, I'll go and get Jimmy, he called Belfast this afternoon." There was a short pause then Declan's twin picked up the phone.

"Afternoon Jonathon, I was going to call you later. I spoke to one of my cousins earlier, our family originally comes from Belfast you know."

"Yes I did know that Jimmy. What did he have to say?" Jonathon smiled to himself – Jimmy was not the sharpest tool in the box but you would definitely want to have him on your side in a fight. Declan was the brains of their company, Jimmy was the muscle, and they were incredibly close and fanatically loyal to each other. Jonathon had been introduced to the McConnells by another of his ex-clients back from his PDS days in Swansea. At the time, they were part of a small gang of drug dealers in Liverpool and Jonathon recognised the twins' potential and set them up in the new transport business as the main hub in his burgeoning supply network.

"Duggan is very well connected and mixes with some serious villains Jonathon, I don't think you could get at him in Ireland. He comes over to Liverpool on the ferry now and again for business and he always has Mick O'Hare with him. Our Fergus says O'Hare is Duggan's partner and bodyguard and definitely not someone to tangle with – he shoots first and asks questions later if you know what I mean."

"I have heard that before about Mr O'Hare and yes I know exactly what you mean Jimmy. If that's the case and it would be difficult to get to Duggan over there, then perhaps we will have to try and bring him to us. Thank you Jimmy, could I have a quick word with your brother please?"

"Yes, no problem. Declan, Jonathon wants a word. Cheers Jonathon." With that, he handed the phone back to his brother and left the office.

"Declan, it seems that Mr Duggan is not an easy man to track down and we may need to change our tactics. Do you think you could entice him over to Liverpool for a chat? Perhaps he would be interested in getting involved in our little distribution network, opening a new Irish office as it were? If your cousin could get a message to him offering a meet up with yourself and Jimmy to discuss the possibilities, he would choose the time and place of course, he might be tempted, he is a businessman after all," Jonathon said with a wry smile. "Obviously you do not mention my involvement at all, and also don't mention Peter Boston unless you feel you have to. Just say that your employer is looking for potential new markets and that your cousin mentioned his name as a possible contact over there. I will clear it with Peter – you never know, Mr Duggan could prove an asset to us after all," Jonathon joked. ('And he could repay some of the money he owes me,' thought Jonathon to himself.) "Keep it vague, see if he is interested. We are just trying to open up a line of communication with him initially."

"I don't suppose you want to tell me what this is all about Jonathon?" asked Declan.

"Just let us say that Mr Duggan has caused me some problems in the past regarding another business venture I was involved in and I am reviewing my options. But you should treat it as a genuine opportunity for us to expand into Ireland and discuss the matter with him accordingly. I'll leave it with you. Let me know if you are able to set anything up." With that, they said their goodbyes and ended the call.

The solicitor then called through to his Office Manager. "Tricia, see if you can get hold of Peter Boston for me."

Shortly after, his internal phone rang. "He's out of the office at the moment, Mr Underwood, but I have left a message for him to ring you."

"Thanks, Tricia."

Thirty minutes later his company mobile rang and Peter Boston's name appeared on the phone's screen.

"Afternoon Peter, thank you for returning my call so promptly. I trust you are well?" Jonathon asked cheerily.

"Yes thanks, Jonathon. What can I do for you?" the Managing Director of Boston Heating & Ventilation Supplies Limited replied.

"Would it be possible to meet up soon for a chat? I may have a new business opportunity to run past you. If you are free tomorrow morning, perhaps we could meet up at the Hartshead Moor services near Bradford on the M62. I could be there for about 11am on the westbound side," suggested Jonathon.

"Yes okay, that's fine by me. See you then," answered Peter and ended the call.

"Tricia, I am going to be out of the office tomorrow morning meeting Peter but should be back in again later in the afternoon," Jonathon advised her.

As arranged, Jonathon met Peter Boston at the services at 11am the following day. After getting a large cappuccino each, they took a table in the general seating area as far away from everyone else as possible.

"Peter, have you ever considered extending your customer base to Ireland?" Jonathon asked after they had exchanged the usual pleasantries.

"No," he answered. "I don't have any contacts and I certainly wouldn't want to step on anyone's toes over there by trying to muscle in on their territory."

"Fully understand old chap, very sensible approach. However, I may be able to set up someone who would act as a middleman between you and whoever is the main man over there, purely in a 'supplier only' capacity of course. He is local and very well connected and not in the trade directly himself so would be ideal. Also, there would be little risk as you would simply be delivering the goods to him and not having to get involved in the distribution. What do you think?"

"Sounds interesting Jonathon," Peter answered thoughtfully. "Our European partners are always pushing for us to take more product and our current network is pretty much at saturation point so it would be possible as long as our buy-in and sell-on prices were right. I presume the McConnells would handle the transportation across to where, Dublin, Belfast or Larne?"

"Yes they would but we haven't decided the route as yet, that would be down to the contact over there. So you're okay with the general idea then?" Jonathon asked. Peter nodded in agreement. "Excellent, I won't move on anything without consulting you first of course Peter."

They stood up and shook hands like any ordinary businessmen after a successful meeting and went their separate ways.

When Jonathon got back into his two-year-old black BMW 7 series, he immediately rang Declan McConnell on his company mobile. Declan answered on the third ring, seeing Jonathon's name appear on the screen. "Afternoon, Jonathon."

"Afternoon Declan, I've just come out of a meeting with Peter and he is happy for you to contact our friend in Ireland. I'll leave it with you." Jonathon ended the call and smiled.

Chapter 14

Jonathon and Abigail arrived at the Mere Golf Resort & Spa promptly at 7pm for the champagne reception prior to the main gala charity dinner on behalf of the British Heart Foundation at 8pm. It was one of many such charitable events organised throughout the year by Abigail and her friends, all members of the very wealthy "Cheshire Set", although this event had special meaning to Abigail as her father had died of a heart attack just over ten years ago.

There were 80 tables, each seating ten guests and costing £10,000 per table. There would be various fundraisers throughout the evening including the stand-up bingo which was always popular and great fun as an initial ice-breaker, the silent auction for a two-week holiday in the Maldives and a live auction of various donated goodies. After the meal, a couple of Premier League footballers and a well-known retired football manager, who were regulars at such events as they lived locally on "millionaires row" across from the Mere, had offered to sign the evening's menu at £100 a time for the charity. There was also a "golden post-box" where attendees could "deposit" cheque donations anonymously.

The evening was a black tie and evening dress occasion and the rich and famous were out in force displaying a wide range of designer haute couture and sparkling jewellery.

Jonathon loved such occasions, with his beautiful wife on his arm dressed in a stunning Christian Lacroix dress which was complemented by the beautiful emerald necklace and matching diamond and emerald earrings he had "bought" her for her recent birthday, which had in actual fact been manufactured and supplied direct from his anonymously owned exclusive jewellery shop on Oxford Road in Manchester. He mingled effortlessly with the other guests, swapping small talk with people he did not know personally but knew by reputation whilst trying to guess which of the ladies were also wearing some of the exclusive, bespoke jewellery he supplied at his very popular retail outlet which his darling wife had innocently recommended to many of her wealthy girlfriends. At 8pm, the Master of Ceremonies called everyone to their seats and, as Jonathon went to the table he was sponsoring, he noticed Brian and Joanna Mather and Joanna's father William at an already full table.

"Well this is a surprise Brian, I didn't know you were coming this evening," Jonathon said as he approached them and stopped. "Brian, Joanna, this is my wife Abigail, I don't think you've met? Abigail, this is Brian and Joanna Mather who own Wade Manufacturing, one of my clients, and this is William, Joanna's father and former Managing Director."

"Hi Brian, Joanna, William, great to meet you all. Pleased you could come and support tonight's event," Abigail replied, giving them all a salutary peck on the cheek.

"Abigail is one of tonight's organisers," Jonathon said proudly. "Have you sponsored the table or are you a guest

Brian?"

"We were invited by Bill," Brian replied.

William smiled and nodded in acknowledgement as they all sat back down.

"Good to see you again William," replied Jonathon, smiling. "The company is obviously doing well if you can afford to sponsor a table," he continued jokingly.

"I'm just a guest as well. The sponsor is my good friend and golf partner here at Mere, Leo Bright," William said, pointing at the man sitting down next to him. Leo stood up and held out his hand to Jonathon.

"Pleased to meet you, Jonathon," he said as they shook hands.

"Are you in business Leo or retired?" Jonathon asked politely.

"Sorry, Jonathon," interjected William, "I should have introduced you properly. Leo is the Chief Constable of the Cheshire Police Constabulary."

"Off duty of course, I hasten to add," Leo added with a smile.

Jonathon froze for a split second holding onto Leo's hand but quickly regained his composure and joked, "We're in a similar line of business then – you catch them and I defend them, if they are innocent of course."

"Bill tells me you were originally with the Public Defender's Service down in Swansea for a few years before you came up to Manchester," the Chief Constable replied.

"Yes, just over eleven years," Jonathon confirmed.

"Do you play golf Jonathon? Perhaps we could have a fourball with Bill and Brian at Mere sometime?" suggested the Chief Constable.

"No, sorry, afraid I have never played Leo. Lovely to meet you, please excuse us we must find our table," replied Jonathon as he took his wife's arm and led her to their places at the front of the hall near the small stage where the various prizes and auction lots were displayed along with a microphone on a stand.

As they sat down, the Master of Ceremonies took to the stage and lifted the microphone.

"Ladies and gentlemen, welcome to the annual gala dinner on behalf of the British Heart Foundation here at the fabulous Mere Golf Resort & Spa. Before we settle down, please could I ask you all to stand for our first event of the evening – the ever-popular 'stand up bingo'. I'm sure you all know how this works. In front of each place setting is a small bingo card. I will call out a number randomly selected from the board in front of me and if that number matches any of the ones on your bingo card you can sit down. The last person standing is the winner of this lovely jeroboam of Dom Perignon vintage champagne, kindly donated by the Mere Resort. So let's get the evening under way," he concluded and picked the first number.

Jonathon sat down on the third number called and took the opportunity to Google the Chief Constable of the Cheshire Constabulary on his iPhone. He was soon looking at a photograph of Leonard Harrison Bright with a short biography. Abigail sat down shortly afterwards so Jonathon closed the page and put his phone away.

Jonathon put his new acquaintance out of his mind and settled down to enjoy the evening which proved to be a great success, the food and company were excellent. The event set a new record for the amount raised by the Foundation at Mere: the final sum donated, including the cheques from the golden post box and after taking off all the expenses and costs, was just short of £1.2 million so the evening was heralded as a great success and Abigail's committee looked forward to presenting the cheque to the British Heart Foundation.

When Jonathon finally returned home in the early hours of Sunday morning, he texted Brian Mather. "I didn't know you moved in such exalted circles, you must tell me more about your friend the Chief Constable when we next meet."

Jonathon's phoned vibrated almost immediately. "Didn't know Bill knew him, never mind played golf with him. Complete shock when he introduced us to him when we first arrived. Speak later."

Chapter 15

The retired Detective Chief Inspector took up his position at 7pm on the Tuesday evening following his last meeting with Steve Guest. He was just above Eglwys Siglen rocks, opposite Ynys Moelfre, the small island that was a haven for nesting cormorants, shags and seagulls and that short line of coast that led down to the locally named Mackerel Rock which was extremely popular with both local and visiting fishermen. It afforded him a perfect view of the coastline behind Plas Meirion in both directions, to both Lligwy and Dulas Bays to the left and Moelfre and Benllech to the right. He had been a keen fisherman in the past and had done quite a bit of night-time fishing so it was the perfect cover for observing their quarry without raising any suspicions. He had all the necessary warm waterproof clothing and fishing tackle to hand and he was looking forward to renewing his old hobby – he just hoped the weather would be kind to him and stay mainly dry.

They had decided that John would keep watch on Tuesday and Thursday nights – those were the most likely times that something might happen as it was on Wednesdays and Fridays that the delivery man drove into the Manchester offices of Wade's. As Steve's wife had already queried his recent nightly exploits, following on from his other nocturnal outings when he had rented the cottage while he was watching for any possible roadside activity from Plas Meirion, they thought it best if he did not arouse any further suspicion by sharing the new nocturnal outings.

The first night of watching passed without incident, either any suspicious activity over behind Plas Meirion or by catching any fish. The weather stayed dry and John returned home at first light having enjoyed renewing his old sea-fishing hobby.

It was the same for the Thursday and the following two Tuesdays and Thursdays, other than being joined on a couple of occasions by some fellow anglers who also enjoyed the same night-time pastime. The weather had stayed mainly fine except for the second Tuesday when a particularly heavy storm swept through and John returned home the following morning thoroughly cold, wet and miserable. But a change into some warm clothes, a mug of hot tea followed by a full plate of sausage, bacon, egg, beans and toast soon cheered him up and after an hour reading the paper, he went to bed to catch up on some of his lost sleep, waking up several hours later fully refreshed both in body and mind.

He was finally rewarded for his perseverance three weeks after the first overnight vigil on the rocks opposite Ynys Moelfre. As usual, he had set up his fishing rod on the fourth Tuesday evening just after 7pm and settled down for the nightly vigil. It had just turned 2am when he heard a muffled throbbing sound coming from the other side of the island and moving towards his left and Lligwy Bay, the direction of

Plas Meirion. During the previous nights, the occasional fishing boat had passed to and fro behind the small island but their engine noises were much louder and clearer – it was the quieter, less distinct sound that had attracted John's attention this night. When he took out the night vision binoculars he had recently bought, he quickly zeroed into a small dinghy containing two men heading round the bay. There were a couple of other fishermen just down from John so he was confident that even if the men in the small boat saw him it would not raise any suspicions about his presence. He followed them with the binoculars for about a few hundred metres. They then turned sharply left towards the shore until they disappeared out of sight below the cliffs by an inlet that John knew was the entrance to a small pebble beach just below where Plas Meirion backed onto the coast.

Nothing further happened until about fifteen minutes later when the small dinghy reappeared and the two men started to retrace their route back towards the far side of the island opposite John. Rounding the back of the island, they reappeared almost immediately on the other side, heading out to sea and making John wonder where they were going in such a small craft. He soon got his answer when they approached one of the large ships that often anchored in the bay opposite Moelfre, either sheltering from bad weather or awaiting their arrival slot at Liverpool harbour or the refineries at Runcorn and Stanlow. He marked the ship's position and, to keep up his cover, waited for first light before noting the name *MV Caracas* and returning home for a well-deserved hot mug of tea and a cooked breakfast.

As soon as he got back in, he texted Steve: "Bingo. Follow him as agreed. Take extra care and see you at the pub tonight." They had agreed that if John spotted anything suspicious during the night he would let Steve know, who would then follow the delivery driver at a very safe distance to check if he made any unscheduled stops on his usual route into Wade's. Steve knew the route he normally took as both he and John had already followed him at a very discreet distance on a couple of earlier occasions, so he would be able to keep a very healthy distance between himself and the white Transit to avoid any possibility of the driver spotting him.

Steve was in position in the lay-by-cum-bus-stop opposite the turning to Marian-Glas in plenty of time before Mathew Dawson, complete with the latest consignment of smuggled gemstones from Nigeria, drove past just after 9.30am as usual on his way into Manchester. It was a very straightforward journey, taking the A5025 through Benllech and Pentraeth before dropping down onto the A55 and crossing over the Menai Straits on the Britannia Bridge. It was then a straight road on the A55 and A494 through Queensferry all the way to the M56 into Manchester, picking up the M60 westbound and coming off at Junction 9 onto the A5081 for Trafford Park. Wade Manufacturing Limited was just down to the roundabout, second exit and about 200 metres on the left-hand side. Steve knew the route well and so was able to keep well back as Mathew followed his normal routine, arriving two hours later at the main gate before going through to the warehouse as usual. Steve had already found a side road on a previous reconnoitre back towards the roundabout where he could park up and watch out for Mat's return. Mathew duly exited the main gate one and a half hours later and returned to Moelfre by exactly the same route in reverse without any unscheduled stops or detours.

When Steve arrived home, he immediately texted John: "Mission accomplished, see you later," and then settled down for the long wait until their prearranged meeting later that evening.

They entered the pub together at five to seven that evening with supressed excitement and expectation. Steve went to the bar while John picked a table at the back of the lounge to ensure they were unlikely to be accidentally overheard by anyone. Steve picked up the two pints and took them over to John and opened the conversation before he had sat down. "What happened last night?" he asked eagerly.

"I'll come to that in a moment," John replied. "Did Mathew go straight to Wade's? Any unscheduled stops on the way there or back?" he continued.

"No, everything was as usual," Steve confirmed. "He went straight to the warehouse and then came out about ninety minutes later and went back home to Moelfre, no detours."

"Right, that means he is probably taking whatever it is to someone at Wade's, possibly his boss, the Transport Manager John Bootle, he has to be in on it as well. What we have to find out now, if we can, is what it is and what happens to it next," John confirmed.

"What happened last night?" Steve repeated.

"What do you see out of the front window of the pub? You've sat there enough," asked John obliquely.

"What do you mean?" replied Steve. "What's that got to do with anything?"

"Just answer the question," smiled John.

"Alright, you've got the bay, Puffin Island, in the distance there's the Great Orme by Llandudno on the mainland and then sea all the way to Ireland."

"What else is there?" John pressed.

"Nothing," said Steve in exasperation, having no idea where John was trying to lead him.

"Exactly!" exclaimed John. "We look but we do not see. If you had asked me that question, my reply would have been exactly the same as yours and I have been coming in here a lot longer than you. What there is, every day and night almost without exception, is a number of large ships temporarily anchored in the bay – always has been as long as I can remember. It is a perfect place for ships sheltering from bad weather or simply waiting their turn to dock at the various ports up and down the coast near here and nobody takes the slightest bit of notice of them. It's a perfect cover if someone on board one of them wanted to deliver some clandestine cargo locally – hiding in plain sight. Last night, around 2am, a small dinghy with two men left the *MV Caracas* anchored out in the bay behind Moelfre Island and I watched them head towards Lligwy beach before turning in towards shore, presumably to land at that pebble beach at the back of Plas Meirion. About fifteen minutes later, they reappeared and returned to their own ship which means that they only had time to go up to the bungalow and drop something off before quickly returning." John paused and took a long drink from his pint.

"So," concluded Steve, "at least we have now confirmed what we suspected – there is something very suspicious going on at Plas Meirion and it definitely concerns Wade's and almost certainly the Manchester solicitor. What do we do now?"

"Very good question Steve. At some stage, we are going to have to go to the police with all this, but as yet we have no proof, just circumstantial evidence involving a very superficial old investigation, some very suspicious night-time activity and lots of coincidences, however compelling they may be when considered as one linked conspiracy. And there's also the big question of who do we tell? It certainly can't be Colwyn Bay police where Charlie Watkins is stationed and probably not the Manchester force either as we don't know who else might be involved with the solicitor."

The two friends went back over what they had seen over the last twenty-four hours, trying to understand how it all might fit in with the original mystery surrounding the missing Peter Ainsworth from Plas Meirion, the very suspicious dealings of the Manchester solicitor and the clandestine visit of the two sailors to the bungalow at Moelfre in the middle of the night. A couple of pints later, having got no further towards any sort of conclusions, they decided to call it a night and sleep on it and meet up the following evening to discuss their next move.

Chapter 16

Twenty-four hours later, they were back in their usual seats at the window of the pub, each with a pint of their favourite drink in front of them. The retired policeman had drawn up a brief list of all the facts and some informed guesses regarding their investigations to date. They agreed, after reviewing them all and after much further discussion, that they needed a lot more information regarding whatever was going on at Plas Meirion, Wade's and the solicitor's and how it all linked to the original disappearance of Peter Ainsworth before they could take their suspicions to the police. They also reluctantly agreed that they were at a bit of a dead end with their efforts to discover what was happening at Plas Meirion. Yes, they knew that something illegal was almost certainly being delivered there from the *Caracas* and then on to Wade's, but they had no way of finding out what it was and where it went afterwards or who else was involved.

"I think we are going to have to change the emphasis of our investigation again Steve," John Wyn Thomas concluded. "The key to all this is the solicitor Jonathon Underwood, everything we know revolves around him."

Steve nodded. "Yes, I agree."

"So, let's leave Wade's and the goings on in Moelfre out of it for now and see if we can link Underwood into all this and go after him instead."

"Okay, that sounds good to me," Steve confirmed.

"According to my private investigator friend, the first firms he was involved with after his move to Manchester were Boston's out at Hull and the transport company at Liverpool and they happened around the same time. He also mentioned that there was a local rumour that the main man at Boston's had previously been involved in the local drug trade but nothing had ever been proven and it was supposedly only small-time stuff anyway. Underwood did not get involved with Wade's until several years later so it is not an unrealistic assumption to think that he probably started what we believe to be his illegal activities a lot earlier and it could well have been with Boston's. So I propose we try and find out more about Peter Boston and his heating and ventilating supplies company and if and how they are tied in with Underwood's Liverpool company."

"Sounds good, John. What about Wade's though? Are you suggesting we forget about them for the time being?"

"No, I think you should still keep an eye on Plas Meirion – or, more precisely, on the bay and see when that ship re-appears and if there are more deliveries to the bungalow, when and how often. It can't have been just a one-off, it must be a regular occurrence to justify all the money and effort that has been put into it. When it does show up, let me know and I will take up position again to see if a delivery takes place. Meanwhile, I will try and make contact with someone over at Hull, ideally a retired ex-copper like myself who has some good local knowledge. I will need to be careful because we don't know who might be involved over there, especially if Underwood has someone on his payroll at the local station like he does over here. I'll see if one of my old colleagues at Colwyn Bay can put me in touch with someone who fits the bill at Hull and hope we don't set off alarm bells anywhere."

Having agreed their new course of action, they finished their drinks and left together with a new sense of purpose.

The following morning, John Wyn Thomas called an old friend from the traffic division, someone he had known from well before the suspect Detective Sergeant Charlie Watkins had moved to North Wales, someone who was very unlikely to know Watkins or be involved in any possible conspiracy. He told the police officer he was thinking of writing a book about drug trafficking and was looking to do some background work around probable ports of entry into the UK. John asked him to keep it to himself for the time being as he was at the early stages of the possible project and what he was looking for was perhaps a retired officer who had been involved in that kind of investigation over at Hull. The officer said he would make a few calls and get back to him.

A few hours later, John's mobile rang: it was the traffic officer returning his call. "Afternoon John, you're in luck. I called a guy from Traffic I met at a course recently from over there and he's given me the name and number of a detective sergeant who was on the Drugs task force for about five years and retired earlier this year. His name is Andy Cauldwell and he was based at the Humberside headquarters on Priory Road in Hull. Got some paper and a pen?"

John took a note of his contact details, thanked him for his help and again asked him to keep his enquiry completely confidential and not to mention it to anyone. He immediately rang the number of the retired detective sergeant and introduced himself, using the book story to set up a meeting the following week with the ex-drugs investigator who was only too happy to talk to John, one former detective to another.

The two retired detectives met the following Tuesday lunchtime, coincidentally at the same motorway services on the M62 near Bradford and in the same dining area where Jonathon Underwood had met Peter Boston a couple of weeks earlier. After the initial introductions, they chatted generally about their respective police careers and their retirements before John guided the conversation around to the purpose of the meeting. He gave Andy a vague outline of his fictitious book and asked him if he could give him any general background about the drugs trade down the North-East coast, reassuring him that anything he said was strictly "off the record" and that he would not use any names or specific incidents, he was just after general background. Although the ex-drugs investigator was happy to chat with John, he was very aware that he had to be careful what he told him, fellow ex-detective or not, so he too kept the information very vague and included nothing that couldn't be found with a little research on the internet or through the local papers or court records. John let him continue with this for a short while before casually mentioning the real object of his enquiries.

"A name I came across while I was involved in an investigation before I retired, someone who was based over your way, was a guy called Peter Boston. Mean anything to you? It was to do with a haulage company over in Liverpool which we thought might be involved in some drugs trafficking in North Wales. We were never able to prove anything but they made regular trips to and from Boston's company in Hull," volunteered John, hoping he had guessed right and that there was a tie-up between the two Underwood companies and drugs.

"I wondered how long it would be before you got round to the real reason you asked for this meeting," smiled Andy.

"What do you mean?" asked a surprised John Wyn Thomas.

"Background for a book on drug trafficking and coming all the way over here? Not very credible really."

"Was it that transparent?" asked John, embarrassed by his apparently weak cover story. "Okay," he said, quickly changing tack, "tell me about yourself, where you were born, where you have lived, how long in the force, that sort of thing," he continued, trying to buy himself some time while he decided how much he could divulge to this stranger who, after all, could be involved.

"What's that got to do with anything?" Andy replied aggressively.

"Sorry, but you caught me off guard. Please just humour

me for the moment," John answered him. "Once I know a little bit more about you, I'll tell you as much as I can. I would really appreciate it."

Andy's interest aroused, he was happy to reply to John's strange request. "Okay, fair enough. After all, you have come a long way so I presume it is quite important," Andy smiled, deflating the tension which had suddenly sprung up between them.

"I was born in Bridlington and lived there with my mum and dad before joining the army straight from school after my A levels. Served in the Royal Engineers for just under five years, including my basic training at Catterick. Decided it wasn't for me so handed my papers in and left. Didn't have a clue what I wanted to do and ended up joining the police in Humberside after being on the dole for six months. Started at the bottom as a beat bobby, worked my way up to Sergeant before transferring across to the Detective division where I spent the next twenty years, the last five with the Drugs Taskforce. Retired last summer. Married once, divorced after ten years, no kids and a springer spaniel called Ben. That do you?"

John decided very quickly that he liked this man and was confident that he could trust him so he gambled and asked him, "Ever heard of a Jonathon Underwood, Andy?"

"No, should I have?" Andy answered.

"Or Detective Sergeant Charlie Watkins?" John continued.

"Again, no," Andy replied.

"Finally, any links with Swansea? Personally, through work

or through family?"

"Definitely not," responded Andy smiling. "Closest I've been is Abersoch in a caravan on holiday and it rained for the entire week."

John had been watching Andy very carefully to see if there was any hint of recognition in his eyes when he mentioned the two names and he was certain his reactions and his answers were completely genuine. John decided to take his new acquaintance into his confidence and tell him the real reason why he had travelled over 140 miles to meet him.

"Okay, I think we should go and sit in one of the cars and I'll tell you what I know and what I want to do about it," the Welsh ex-Detective Chief Inspector said. So they left the dining area and went outside and both got into Andy's metallic grey Vauxhall Astra. John then spent the next thirty minutes telling Andy everything he knew about their investigations so far and all the different people and companies involved. After John finished, Andy just sat there in complete silence for what seemed like an age, before finally coming out of his reverie. "Wow, that's some story John for sure. And I agree – when you put it all together with Underwood in the middle it certainly looks like he could be at the centre of one big, illegal organisation."

"Do you think Boston's could be involved with drugs?" interrupted John hopefully.

"If they are, we don't know anything about it. Also, from what you say, it might be on quite a big scale and if what you suspect is true then that is even more worrying – the fact that we are completely unaware of it. I would love to help you and get involved."

"I was hoping you were going to say that Andy. We need something concrete before we take this to the authorities and your local knowledge and inside contacts could be key. But we need to be careful, we don't know who else from the force might be involved."

"I agree, leave it with me for the moment and I'll see what I can find out."

With that, the two ex-detectives agreed to speak again soon and John went back to his own car and then drove back to Anglesey, happy with the new addition to their unofficial investigation team.

As soon as he arrived back in Moelfre, John called Steve and updated him on the day's developments. Steve had nothing new to add – the *MV Caracas* had not reappeared in the bay – but he was also very pleased with the new team member and agreed that Andy would be a very helpful addition to their investigation.

The following afternoon, John Wyn Thomas's mobile rang and his new colleague Andy Cauldwell told him that he had spoken unofficially to one of his trusted ex-colleagues who had indeed confirmed that there was no ongoing investigation into the dealings of Peter Boston's company or any suspicion that he might be involved in anything illegal, including drugs. However, after hearing Andy's suspicions concerning the heating and ventilating supplies company and the Liverpool-based transport firm, he agreed to look closer into their activities whilst being incredibly careful to keep his investigation as confidential as possible. John and Andy had agreed that they would only divulge enough of their suspicions to arouse the interest of the Hull-based detective and would not mention Jonathon Underwood or Wade's, simply relying on his respect for his former colleague and the possibility of him uncovering a large drugs operation.

Chapter 17

Declan and Jimmy McConnell set off early in their white company Transit van to get the 10.30am Stena Line ferry from Birkenhead to Belfast. They had allowed plenty of time in case the tunnel crossing under the Mersey River was busier than usual but the traffic was light and there were no hold ups. The ferry left on schedule and they arrived just over eight hours later at the Belfast ferry terminal on Dargan Road. Through their cousin Fergus, they had arranged to meet Jerry Duggan at a pub in Belfast between 7.30pm and 8pm. Fergus had contacted Duggan through a mutual acquaintance, rather than speaking to him directly, and had promised a potentially lucrative business proposition. Duggan had refused to meet on the mainland and insisted on it taking place in Northern Ireland where he knew he would be in control. The meeting had finally been agreed after Duggan had checked out the McConnells' background and he had stipulated the time and place.

When Declan and Jimmy arrived, Jerry Duggan was already standing at the bar with Mick O'Hare and they immediately picked up their drinks and walked over to a table at the rear of the bar, motioning for Declan and Jimmy to follow them having had a full description of the twins and immediately recognising them.

"It's alright boys, you don't need a drink," stated Jerry, sitting down. "If what you have to say is of interest, we'll be leaving together to discuss it further. If it isn't, you'll be leaving and returning to Liverpool."

The twins both glared at Duggan, taken aback by his blatant rudeness, and then sat down opposite the two Irishmen.

Declan recovered first and smiled at Jerry before putting a gentle restraining hand on his brother's knee and replying, "And good evening to you too Mr Duggan, I presume you are Jerry Duggan?" Jerry nodded in assent. "So you must be Mr O'Hare," he continued, looking at the man sitting next to Jerry. Mick just stared blankly at Declan and made no reply. "This is my brother and partner Jimmy. You are obviously men of few words so I will get straight to the point. My business partner…"

"Your boss, Peter Boston," interrupted Duggan.

"…is interested," continued Declan smoothly, ignoring Duggan's taunt, "in exploring the possibility of expanding our sphere of activities to Ireland, both Northern and the Republic. If you know who my associate is, I presume you know what products we are discussing."

"I do and it's not something I have been involved in," replied Jerry.

"We also have done our research Mr Duggan and that is precisely why we have contacted you. We are not interested in going into competition with the existing suppliers and dealers, simply in providing an additional source of supply if one is required. We have chosen you specifically because you are not involved in the trade but we are informed that you are well connected and we think that you would be an ideal intermediary between ourselves and the relevant parties over here. We would deliver the goods to you here and you would then transfer them to the said third parties. There would be little risk to yourself and the earnings could be substantial."

Declan paused and waited for Duggan's reply. The fact that Jerry already knew about Peter Boston and hence their product, a point which impressed Declan, and had agreed to the meeting told him that he would be interested given the right circumstances. Jerry looked over at Mick O'Hare who gave a slight nod of approval.

"Okay Declan, you have my attention." With that, Jerry and Mick finished their drinks and stood up. "Are you booked on the 10.30pm ferry to Liverpool?" Jerry asked.

"Yes," replied Declan, nodding.

"Right, where are you parked?" the Irishman asked.

"Round the back of the pub, in the car park," Declan replied.

"So are we, the black Range Rover. Follow us, we'll go to Mick's place out towards Larne, it's only about 20 minutes. We can carry on our chat there. You'll have plenty of time to catch the ferry."

The four men left the pub and went round to the car park and got into their respective vehicles. The Transit van followed the Range Rover and 18 minutes later they turned off the main Larne Road onto a farm lane and stopped in front of a large stone farmhouse. During the journey, Declan called Jonathon Underwood and gave the solicitor a brief update on their meeting in the pub and their current destination as Jimmy drove in silence.

"Excellent Declan, try and make a mental note of the layout of everything out there. It could be very useful at a later date if we need to pay our new friends a visit," the solicitor replied and ended the call.

The twins got out of the Transit and followed the two men into the house. They took them through into the kitchen and they all sat down at a large oak dining table where Mick's wife Aileen was already seated. "This is Mick's wife," said Jerry, nodding in Aileen's direction.

"Good evening, Aileen," Declan greeted her, showing that he too knew who he was dealing with.

Jerry smiled in acknowledgement and continued. "As I said, you have my attention. What exactly are you proposing?"

Declan outlined the proposal Jonathon Underwood had discussed with him, which was to offer Duggan a very lucrative incentive to act as the middleman between the Irish drug suppliers and his Hull-based operation. Jonathon had made the terms very favourable to the Irishman as he really had little intention of actually setting up a deal – his main objective was to establish contact, gain his trust and gather as much information about him as possible. After a further short discussion, Duggan confirmed his interest and promised to get back to Declan once he had established through his contacts if there was any interest in Declan's proposals and if so what quantities and which type of drugs would be required. The four men shook hands and the twins left the house, got into their Transit and turned down the lane on their way back to the ferry terminal in Belfast.

Once they were on the main road, Declan broke the silence. "What do you think Jimmy?"

"Wouldn't touch them with a barge pole brother. That guy with Duggan is a nutter, did you see his eyes? He never stopped staring at us. Scary."

"I agree Jimmy. They say it takes one to know one," Declan said jokingly to his twin brother.

With that, he took out his mobile and rang the solicitor in Manchester again as Jimmy drove them back to the ferry port. His call was answered almost immediately.

"How did it go?"

"As expected, Duggan is interested and is going to make enquiries about possible clients and quantities and get back to me."

"Excellent, and what did you think about our potential Gaelic associates?"

"I asked Jimmy the same question."

"And his reply?"

"He wouldn't touch them with a barge pole and he thought O'Hare was scary."

"And your opinion?"

"I agree with Jimmy, especially about O'Hare." He then gave Jonathon a full report of their meeting, both at the pub and then at the farmhouse, including its location and a description and detailed layout of the farmhouse and outlying buildings as requested, something Jonathon was particularly interested in.

"Thank you Declan, your visit has been very useful for me. Have a safe journey back and I'll speak to you shortly. Obviously if you hear back from Duggan, let me know."

Jonathon ended the call and sat back in his office chair thinking about what his next step should be. He often stayed late in Manchester, well after normal office hours, and had told his wife Abigail not to expect him till later that evening. He was not surprised with Declan's review of his meeting with Duggan and his subsequent recommendation not to get involved with him – in fact, he welcomed it because it made his next decision quite straightforward. He smiled as he took one of the PAYG phones out of the top drawer of his desk and dialled the only number that was in the phone's directory. The call was answered after several rings, just before it went to voicemail.

"Hello," a man with a strong South African accent answered.

"Good evening Andre, it is Jonathon Underwood. Sorry for calling so late. Can you speak?"

"Yes," he replied. Andre Botha was an ex-South African policeman who had emigrated from his native country to the UAE after the election of Nelson Mandela as their new president and set up a personnel protection company along with three of his compatriots from similar backgrounds. Through previous contacts in South Africa, his company soon found work as bodyguards to one of the minor members of the royal family. In the last years of his service in Dubai, each spring and summer, most of the royal family and their entourage moved en-masse to London and Newmarket for the Flat Racing Season, the male members attending the various race meetings and the wives shopping in the West End. After many years with the sheik, Andre had grown his business to employ over twenty people and in the early 1990s decided to leave and set up business in London where he could service various summer contracts with his old contacts and also diversify into other areas where his expertise and that of some of his employees could be put to alternative and more lucrative uses.

Andre had been recommended to Jonathon by one of his many contacts from his Public Defenders days when he was having trouble with one of his main dealers in the Midlands. He had arranged a meeting with Andre in London and had been impressed with his smart business-like appearance and professionalism. Andre had laid out his scale of fees depending on what was required as if he were discussing how a diseased tree should be treated and the relevant cost: whether Jonathon required the problem simply superficially handled to serve as a warning, some limbs broken involving hospital time or the problem completely removed.

After Jonathon had confirmed that he required removal, and had given Andre a quick overview of the person concerned complete with contact details and home address, a fee was agreed and half transferred to an offshore account there and then with the remainder on completion. They had enjoyed an excellent meal and before leaving Andre had given Jonathon his private business card. A week later, Jonathon heard that the problem dealer had mysteriously disappeared, never to be heard from again and he quickly replaced him in his organisation. After a confirmatory call from Andre, he happily wired the second half of the fee and promised to get in touch if he ever needed his services again.

"If you are still trading, Andre, I would like to employ your services once again," Jonathon said hopefully.

"I am," Andre replied.

"Excellent. This contract is a lot more complicated but I hope it is within your remit," Jonathon continued. He gave Andre a full outline of the targets, their background and the address of the farmhouse at Larne in Northern Ireland as well as promising to email a full description of the property layout later if required.

"Full removal, including the wife?" Andre asked once Jonathon had finished.

"Yes please and I feel I must stress these are very dangerous people."

"Understood. I will need to do a full reconnaissance of the area and a project feasibility study before I commit to this for which I will need to be fully recompensed whether I go ahead or not."

"Agreed Andre. Just let me know your expenses," confirmed the solicitor.

"And please send me the detailed information regarding

the layout of the farmhouse."

"Will do," answered Jonathon.

"Good, I will be in touch after we have looked into this. If it is a go, I will let you know the price."

"Excellent Andre, I look forward to hearing from you. Have a good evening."

Jonathon ended the call, put the phone back in the drawer, picked up his brown leather Gucci briefcase, locked the office and went to retrieve his car from the private car park before returning home to Wilmslow.

It was three weeks before Jonathon got a return call from Andre as he was finishing his evening meal at home. His private mobile rang and Andre's name appeared on the iPhone screen.

"Good evening Andre, lovely to hear from you," Jonathon said as he stood up from the table and went into his study, mouthing the words 'sorry, work' to his wife Abigail as he went.

"We are happy to go ahead with the contract. The cost will be thirty thousand plus expenses. I will add our costs to-date to the final expenses invoice. We will need a four-man team and they may have to be over there for several days."

"Understood Andre. I will transfer fifteen over shortly. Is it the same account details as previously?"

"Yes. I will be in touch," and Andre ended the call.

Jonathon returned to the table and his wife asked, "Everything alright dear?"

"Oh yes darling. Just a little problem that had been

niggling at me and needed resolving, nothing important. It is all sorted now," replied her husband smiling happily.

The following week, a white Mercedes Sprinter van containing two athletic-looking South African men boarded the P&O Ferry at Cairnryan Port in Stranraer bound for Larne in Northern Ireland. It was followed fifteen minutes later by a Skoda Octavia Estate car with two similarly athletic-looking Geordie lads. Two hours later they arrived at Larne and made their way separately to two different campsites. They had been chosen from the earlier reconnaissance: both were about three miles from the farmhouse at Ballyclare, one to the West near Ballyeaston and one to the North towards Ballynure. They pitched their tents just after 9pm and settled down for the night.

At first light, both pairs were up and off, looking like typical holiday hikers complete with standard outdoor gear and boots but slightly larger backpacks than were normal hiking issue. They went their separate ways to two prearranged observation points about 200 metres from the house, again one to the West and one to the North, giving them a clear view through their powerful binoculars of the front and back of the property. They then settled down to wait. They had no idea when their three targets would meet up together at the farmhouse but they did know that they met at least three or four times a week at different times of the day and evening. But whenever they met, the two teams would be in place and able to take advantage of whatever opportunity presented itself in order to fulfil their contract.

The first day passed without incident. Aileen was at home all day and occasionally appeared outside, going to a couple of the adjacent outbuildings. Mick left in the black Range Rover at about 10am and returned on his own just before 6pm. With no further comings or goings, the four watchers returned to their respective camps at around 9pm. They had plenty of food and water with them so did not need to leave the site or go to any local shops, keeping very much to themselves.

The second day followed very much the same as the first with Aileen at home all day and Mick leaving in the morning and returning on his own in the early evening. But on the third day of their vigil the routine changed and Aileen left with Mick in the morning and the pair returned a couple of hours later with what appeared to be several bags of shopping. At 4pm, two cars appeared going up the lane towards the house, a black 5 series BMW and a silver Audi RS3. The earpieces of the two South Africans who were behind the house came alive. "See the cars?" asked one of their Geordie colleagues who were watching the front of the farmhouse and lane.

"Not yet," one of the South Africans replied.

"There's a black BMW and a silver RS3. Duggan drives a silver RS3. Wonder whose the Beemer is?"

"Sit tight," replied the South African who was the leader of the group. "Let's see what happens. We are only contracted for the three, and we don't want any collateral damage if at all possible."

"Roger that," came the prompt reply.

Five minutes later, across in the farmhouse kitchen, Mick, Aileen, Jerry and their new visitor, Padraig Donahue, were sitting round the large oak table.

"My man is ready to go Jerry. What's the hold up?" asked Padraig.

"Not sure Paddy," replied Duggan. "I called my contact almost two weeks ago and told him we wanted to go ahead with his proposal and what and how much we wanted. He said he would pass it on to his supplier and get back to me. When he called back last week, he said they were having a slight problem with their main supplier in Amsterdam but it should be resolved shortly. Perhaps they are struggling with the amount, I don't know. He said he would get back to me as soon as he had a delivery date."

"This is not a man to let down Jerry, and he doesn't like being messed about. We need to deliver soon or the deal will be off and I will be up a creek without the proverbial paddle and he will want to speak to you as well, if you know what I mean," Padraig continued.

"Okay, okay, I hear you, leave it with me. I'll get back to my man and see what's happening. As soon as I hear anything, I'll give you a call."

"Make it soon for both our sakes Jerry, okay?"

With that, Padraig got up and left the house. As his car was going down the lane, the South African's earpiece crackled into life again. "Black BMW leaving the house, RS3 still parked outside. No further movement outside," the Geordie reported.

"Okay standby. We could be 'go'. Make your way to position Alpha and await further instructions." The earpieces went silent and the four men started towards their respective attack positions, leaving their main backpacks well-hidden but each carrying their much smaller operational packs and weapons.

Fifteen minutes later, after no movement from the farmhouse, the command went out from the lead South African: "Go, go, go," followed by three replies of "Roger that."

Twenty-one minutes later, the contract had been fulfilled – all three targets had been taken out while sitting around the kitchen table, taken completely by surprise and off-guard. The detailed plan of the farmhouse supplied by the McConnells had proved invaluable and had enabled the team to move through the house quickly and quietly.

The team thoroughly searched the farmhouse room by room, finding a large sports bag containing just over £18,000 in bundles of used £20 and £50 notes, a small box of six large uncut gemstones in the main bedroom vanity unit, four basic Nokia 5310 PAYG mobiles in addition to the three iPhones which belonged to the three targets and two HP laptops, all of which they took away with them when they left. They took the bodies out and buried them in shallow graves behind the large barn – unknown to them, only a short distance from where Peter Ainsworth lay a lot deeper down. They drove Jerry's Audi into the barn and parked it next to the Range Rover and Aileen's new Volkswagen Golf. After switching off the electricity, gas and water, they locked all the external doors in the main house and then collected their large backpacks before retracing their tracks to the two campsites. The lead South African then sent a simple text to Andre: "Contract executed."

The following morning, the Sprinter took the 8am ferry back to Scotland and the Skoda followed two hours later on the 10am crossing. They then made their separate ways back to London and by 8pm all four were in a full debrief meeting with their boss after delivering the money, gemstones, phones and laptops to him before going home for a well-earned sleep.

Immediately after the meeting, Andre called Jonathon who was still in his office in Manchester awaiting his call, having been texted earlier by the South African. "The contract was successfully completed this afternoon," he confirmed and then gave Jonathon a full report including what his team had taken from the farmhouse.

"Excellent Andre, a very professional job once again. Please keep the money as a well-earned bonus but I would very much like the gemstones. Please also destroy the phones and laptops, they are of no interest to me and may contain something which connects my organisation to them. The stones are of particular importance as I believe they belong to me and were part of a much larger consignment stolen from me by Duggan previously. I will wire the fifteen thousand now and please let me know your total expenses."

"Thank you Jonathon," Andre replied and ended the call.

Jonathon then took out his private mobile phone and called Declan McConnell. "Good evening Declan, I trust you are well?"

"Yes thanks Jonathon, what can I do for you?" he asked, looking at his watch to confirm the lateness of the call. "No problem I hope?"

"On the contrary old chap – thought I would share some good news with you. The Irish problem has been resolved, you will not be hearing from him again. In fact, forget you ever heard of him. Speak soon." And with that, Jonathon ended the call, locked his office and went home a very happy man.

Chapter 18

Four weeks after meeting up with retired Chief Inspector John Wyn Thomas at the Bradford Services on the M62 and agreeing to look into Peter Boston's possible drug-related activities, Andy Cauldwell called him back with an update on his investigations.

"I am pretty sure your suspicions regarding Boston's are spot on John," Andy began.

"Excellent Andy, what have you found out?" he asked.

"Once a week on a Thursday, a white Ford Luton van with a tail-lift leaves the Boston's yard at around 7am, drives to Hull and catches the 9am ferry to Rotterdam. It arrives back in Hull between 4am and 5am on the Saturday morning from the 5pm Friday ferry from Rotterdam. The driver takes the van back to Boston's and drives it into the warehouse where he is met by Peter. Peter locks the roller doors and they drive away in their own cars.

"Later on, at around 10am on the Saturday morning, Peter Boston and the guy who drove the Luton to Rotterdam arrive back at the yard and they drive the Luton back out of the warehouse and unload about a dozen large crates and boxes which appear to contain heating units and industrial fans, some of which I presume must have the drugs hidden inside. Two white Transits with McConnell Transport &

Warehousing Limited Liverpool on the side appear shortly afterwards and they load three of the crates into one of them and one into the other vehicle. The rest of the crates are loaded back into the Luton and it is moved to the side of the warehouse.

"The Transit with the three crates drives straight back to Liverpool and disappears into one of the McConnell warehouses at their main depot and the other vehicle drives to one of Boston's building sites around Hull, they seem to go to a different site each week. I recognised the driver of the local Hull delivery, he was done for possession with intent to supply drugs a few years ago, so I hung around the sites he visited and there seemed to be quite a few visitors to each site after he arrived. I'm guessing he was handing out new supplies to local dealers."

"What about the Liverpool end?" John asked.

"Sorry, couldn't get close enough to see into their warehouse and there was a lot of coming and going so I wouldn't have been able to see what happened with those three crates anyway," Andy confirmed.

"That's brilliant Andy, it gives us more ammunition when we decide to take our suspicions to the police. I think we are pretty well there, it's just a matter of how we proceed and who we can take it to. Thanks again for all your help and I'll let you know what happens," John concluded.

"No problem mate, I thoroughly enjoyed getting back into a bit of the old cloak and dagger stuff. Good luck with your investigation." With that, they ended the call and John called his friend Steve to bring him up to date with everything Andy had told him. John suggested they meet at the pub the following Tuesday to decide their best way forward as they both agreed they had enough information to tell the police of their suspicions though the big question still remained who to tell. Unfortunately, Steve said he couldn't make that date as he had arranged to play in an annual charity golf day at Mere Golf Club just outside Knutsford with the builder friend from his old golf club, the one who had helped him with the bungalow refurbishment at Trearddur Bay. About a dozen of them go each year he explained, it was a bit of a tradition and it was a good excuse for him to meet up with some of his old pals. So instead they decided to meet up on the following Thursday.

Chapter 19

The following Tuesday evening, John was enjoying a quiet pint down at the pub in Moelfre. He was sitting in his regular chair in the bay window when his phone beeped announcing the arrival of a new text message and disturbing his train of thought as he reflected on the investigations he had been involved in over the last several months. When he opened it, he was surprised to see it was from Steve, his fellow sleuth.

"That's strange," the retired policeman thought when he saw who the message was from, "I thought he was playing golf today. Wonder what he wants?"

The message was brief but quite dramatic: "Hi John, we need to talk ASAP. I will call you tomorrow AM. Steve."

At 9.10 the following morning, John's phone rang announcing the incoming caller as his friend Steve Guest.

"Morning Steve, what's the big news? Did you win the golf yesterday?" John joked.

"No, unfortunately, although we did have a great day and Tom and I came sixth out of the eighty-odd pairs who took part. You will never guess who was sat at our table for the meal after the event?" Steve asked excitedly.

"Henry Kissinger? No? Go on then, surprise me," John replied with little enthusiasm or interest.

"It was a four-ball better-ball pairs event and there were fourteen of us from Brownhill so we had six pairs who played together in three matches and one odd pair, my good friends Alan and Haydn, who were partnered with a pair from another club which happened to be the host club, Mere. After the round, we all sat down together for a meal and Alan and Haydn invited their partners to join us, which they did," Steve began.

"I presume you are going to get round to telling me the point of all this Steve?" John asked.

"The twelve of us were already seated when Alan, Haydn and their two guests came to our table," Steve continued, "and Alan introduced them to us as Bill and Leo from Mere and they sat down next to me with Haydn on their other side."

"Well this is all very riveting, Steve," John said, by now getting a little irritated with the slowly unfolding story as he had no interest in golf, golfing personalities or any other well-known personalities which he presumed was where Steve's story was leading.

"When they were seated," Steve continued, undeterred, "I got talking to Bill and he introduced himself fully as William Wade, the former owner and now Non-Executive Director of Wade Manufacturing and his playing partner was Leonard Bright, the Chief Constable of the Cheshire Constabulary. I nearly choked on my soup."

"Good God Steve – what an incredible coincidence!" John exclaimed.

"Exactly," Steve agreed.

"Did you say anything to him about our investigations?" John asked nervously.

"Absolutely not! In fact, I was so shocked I didn't say much at all. They must have thought I was very poor company but fortunately Alan and Haydn chatted to them throughout the meal. However, I did manage to have the presence of mind to ask Bill for his mobile number on the premise of perhaps getting in touch sometime in the future to arrange another round of golf at Mere. One thing that did strike me as strange was that he was quite reticent to discuss his company's apparent success and growth over the last few years, something that most businessmen are always very proud and keen to do."

"You're right Steve – we need to have a think about this and discuss how we proceed. This opens up a potential new avenue for us. See you at the pub tomorrow about eight." With that, they finished the call.

Chapter 20

John was already sitting at their usual table when Steve arrived at the pub at 8pm the following evening. He bought himself a pint and took his place across the table from his friend.

"Alright, Steve?" John asked.

"Yes good thanks, you?" replied Steve.

"Fine, didn't sleep much last night," John said.

"Me neither, John. What do you think?"

"What was your opinion of Wade?" the ex-Chief Inspector asked. "Do you think he might be involved?"

"That's the big question isn't it," agreed Steve. "If we go to him and he is part of it, we will have blown it and no doubt they will close down whatever it is they are doing and warn off Underwood and even perhaps take more drastic action against us."

"That is indeed the question, Steve. So what do you think?" John asked again.

"I have spent most of the night and all day today thinking about it and I think he is not involved. Like you've said before, I think Underwood is the main man in all this, along with the accountant. I think they use companies which trade legally but have some people within those companies who work for them and help with their illegal activities in conjunction with the normal legal business. I do not see Bill Wade being involved in anything that is remotely criminal but I cannot be sure."

"That's what I hoped you were going to say," replied John. "I agree with you that it is very unlikely he is involved. I've done a bit of research about Bill and he appears to be very "old school". He comes up clean every time and I would very much doubt that someone involved in criminal activity would be a long-time friend and golf partner of the Chief Constable," John concluded.

"So what do you suggest?" asked Steve hopefully.

"I think you should give him a call now and pass him over to me and I'll try and feel him out and perhaps we could arrange to meet up with him. If he is clean, he could help us put the investigation onto an official footing, especially with the help of his golf partner, if he is so inclined," John suggested.

"Okay, let's give it a go," agreed Steve.

With that, he took out his phone and William Wade's business card and rang his mobile number. The phone rang several times and then went to voicemail so Steve left a short message apologising for the lateness of the call, reminding Bill that they had met at Mere the other night after the golf, leaving his mobile number and asking him if he would call him back as there was something he would like to discuss.

Twenty minutes later, Steve's mobile rang. "Hello, Steve Guest," he answered.

"Hello Steve, it's Bill Wade from Mere Golf Club

returning your call. Sorry I missed you but I was just driving back from the Club. What can I do for you?"

"Good evening Bill, thanks for calling back. I hope it isn't too late. Can you chat?" Steve asked.

"No problem. Just poured myself a tot and having a relax. Fire away," Bill replied.

"It is nothing to do with golf, it's more to do with business, your business in fact. Over the last few months, quite by accident initially, a colleague and I have uncovered some quite concerning activities relating to Wade's and someone related to your company," Steve started cautiously.

"What do you mean?" asked the now alert and very concerned Non-Executive Director.

"Let me pass you over to my colleague, retired Detective Chief Inspector John Wyn Thomas," Steve replied and quickly passed the phone to his friend.

"Good evening Bill. Sorry to call you at home but we thought it would be the best course of action to let you know what we have found out before going directly to the police with it all, which we were about to do when Steve fortuitously bumped into you at your club the other night," John started cautiously.

"What are you suggesting? That Wade's is somehow operating illegally? Because I can assure you that is not the case and never has been. I would be very careful what you accuse us of if I were you," Bill replied angrily.

"Absolutely not Bill. This is not Wade's the company we are talking about, just certain personnel within it and also associated with your firm," John quickly replied, trying to calm Bill down. "If possible, we would like to meet up with you, outline our findings and agree a plan on how best to proceed," he continued.

"Do you think this could result in legal proceedings against us? Should I get legal advice?" Bill asked.

"I doubt whether your company would be prosecuted if what we believe is correct, although legal advice would certainly be useful to you, but not until after we have told you what we know. Perhaps you could invite your friend Leo to our meeting, if you agree to it, but that is up to you," John concluded and waited hopefully for Bill's reply.

After a short pause, Bill replied: "Yes, let's meet up. When and where do you suggest? Obviously it needs to be somewhere private. Are you on Anglesey with Steve?"

"Yes, we both live in Moelfre. How about somewhere halfway between us?" John asked.

"Actually, I've never been to Anglesey and I believe the coastline and views over Snowdonia are stunning. How about I come over to you?" Bill suggested.

"That would be fine if you are okay with travelling here. I live on my own so you could come to my place, it would be completely private and we would have no interruptions. When could you make it?" John asked.

"How about early next week, one lunchtime perhaps?" Bill suggested.

"Tuesday would be fine with me," John said, looking at Steve who nodded in agreement.

"Right, that's agreed. If you could get Steve to text me your full address and postcode I'll see you both next Tuesday around 12 o'clock." With that, Bill ended the call and sat quietly for another hour reflecting on what he might learn the following week, having refilled his whiskey glass.

Back at the pub in Moelfre, Steve and John went back over all the things they had seen and discovered and excitedly looked forward to their meeting with William Wade on the following Tuesday.

Chapter 21

At 9.15am the day before the call between John, Steve and Wade's ex-Managing Director, Jonathon Underwood entered his office, locked the door and called his secretary on the intercom. "Good morning Tricia, I trust you are well."

"Yes fine thanks, Mr Underwood," she replied.

"No calls or interruptions please for the next hour," Jonathon instructed her. He ended the call and reached into the top drawer of his desk and pulled out one of the several PAYG phones which like most of the others only had one number stored in the contact directory.

As arranged, he called the number of another PAYG phone at 9.30am prompt and it was answered almost immediately.

"Good morning Jonathon, how are things in sunny Manchester?"

"Not very sunny old chap, cold, wet and as miserable as ever," he replied with a smile. "How are you?"

"Fine thanks," replied Emrys, his company accountant and partner in all his legal and illegal activities.

"Excellent. There are two main subjects to discuss Emrys: Boston's and Wade's. Firstly, Boston's. I can confirm, much to your relief I know, that our partnership with them is now finally concluded. The last shipment was received in Hull and distributed by McConnell's last Thursday. If you could authorise the final payment to our European colleagues today, then once we have received the monies from the dealer network you can close that operation down completely. Peter's new partners are in position to take over our commitments and he seems very happy with the new arrangement, especially as he has increased his stake and share of the profits."

"I must admit I will sleep easier now, Jonathon," the accountant sighed. "I know it was your first investment and has proven incredibly profitable but you are so much safer and less exposed without it. After all, it's not as though you need the money now. The more legitimate we become the better it will be for both of us."

"True, but it has not been about the money for a while now as you know. I just love the clandestine business," Jonathon replied, "and unlike you, I have never had any trouble sleeping. We will eventually utilise McConnell's for the additional transportation requirements of the new online business at Wade's, which leads us nicely on to them."

Emrys opened a file on the desk in front of him in his Swansea office. "The purchase of the additional warehousing and office accommodation in Trafford Park has gone through, I wired the initial payment through to their solicitors last week. If everything goes smoothly, I will make the final payment on completion and we should get the keys sometime next month."

"Excellent, Emrys," the solicitor replied. "I have notified

the building contractor who will carry out the necessary alterations and refurbishment, and also our project manager who will contact you as required for all necessary additional payments. Please continue to use Account 1GCM, the Grand Cayman offshore account, for all payments for this project. That about covers everything from my end. Have you anything, Emrys?" Jonathon asked.

"Yes, just a couple of things, well three actually," the accountant replied. "Firstly, I received the quarterly management reports for M1, the spacious three-bedroom apartment on the seafront in Miami Beach, USA, and C1, the large detached bungalow adjacent to the marina on Grand Cayman in the Caribbean". They had bought the two properties the previous year through another of their offshore accounts, this one based in Bermuda, both as an investment but also as potential boltholes if they were ever required to disappear quickly and anonymously. It was done at Emrys's suggestion, indeed insistence, as he had no desire to suffer the fate of his previous employers who both ended up serving long custodial sentences for some of the offences he was now happily committing.

"The management companies have completed furnishing the two properties to our specifications and installing the internet and CCTV at both. I will email you the links and you can monitor the CCTV cameras at both properties through your laptop or phone. Secondly," Emrys continued, "following on from the excellent performance of the jewellery shop in Manchester over the last twelve months, and further to your suggestion and after commissioning a feasibility report, I agree that we should expand that particular business and open an additional store in Leeds."

"Leave that with me Emrys and I will get our Estates Manager to locate suitable premises and get back to you with potential costings," Jonathon suggested.

"And finally," the accountant continued, "just a quick update on our two new ventures, the auction house and the London gallery. Their initial performances over the first eight months are very promising, especially on the legitimate side of their businesses in line with our reduced requirement for washing money now that Boston's is closed. I will of course give you a detailed report when I complete their accounts at year end. So unless you have any questions, Jonathon, that wraps it up for me."

"No I think that about covers it for now Emrys. Have a good day and speak to you soon." They completed the call and Jonathon placed the phone back in the desk drawer. He then called through to his secretary, "Any calls Tricia?"

"Just Brian Mather confirming your appointment at 2pm on Thursday."

'Excellent,' thought Jonathon, 'must be this month's delivery from Nigeria.' "Thank you Tricia, I will be leaving the office shortly for the rest of the day. Call me on the mobile if you need me." With that, Jonathon placed a file, his two mobiles and his laptop in his briefcase and left the office.

Chapter 22

Steve Guest arrived at John Wyn Thomas's bungalow at 11.30am, eagerly looking forward to their visit from William Wade to discuss what they had uncovered so far and hopefully to proceed to a full official investigation of Jonathon Underwood and all his business operations. John made them both a coffee and they sat in silence looking out of the large bay window, admiring the fabulous view over the hills to Snowdonia and looking expectantly every few minutes at the hallway leading to the front door. Just after 12pm they heard footsteps leading up to the door and the doorbell rang. John quickly stood up and went to the front door while Steve stood up but stayed where he was in front of his chair. John opened the door and saw two men standing in front of him. The smaller of the two held out his hand and said, "Good afternoon, I'm Bill Wade and this is my friend Leo Bright. I presume you are John Wyn Thomas. Very pleased to meet you." Bill shook John's hand and stepped aside so that Leo could do the same.

"Pleased to meet you both and thanks for coming down." He ushered them through the door and closed it after them. "Please come through to the lounge." As they all entered, Steve stepped forward to meet them.

"Good to see you both again," Steve said as he shook

them both by the hand.

"Please sit down," John said as he pointed to the two armchairs. "Would you like a tea or coffee gentlemen?"

"Tea would be fine, white no sugar please" replied Bill.

"Make that two," echoed Leo.

John went into the kitchen to make the drinks.

"I hope you don't mind that I invited Leo along," Bill asked Steve, "but in the circumstances, depending on what you have to say, I thought it would be sensible."

"No problem at all," Steve replied, "in fact I am pleased you did. He could no doubt give us some very good advice on the best way to proceed and hopefully help us in the process. Did you have a good trip down and find us alright?" Steve asked, continuing the conversation while John made their guests' drinks.

"Yes, no problem. It's a lovely drive down the A55 along the coast and the old satnav brought us straight here. Neither of us has been here before and we are both very impressed, the views over Snowdonia are spectacular. Have you been here long?" Bill asked.

"John is local to the area, here and North Wales, but I only moved down to Moelfre last year from Lancashire."

John returned with the two drinks, placed them on the small side tables next to their chairs and then sat down next to Steve on the large sofa.

There was a short silence, then John leaned forward. "Thank you both for coming down and hopefully you will not regret it. I believe we have uncovered, initially quite by accident by Steve, a serious criminal organisation involved at the very least in the distribution of large quantities of drugs and the smuggling of precious gemstones. The reason we have not gone directly to the police with our suspicions is because of who we believe is the main man at the head of the organisation and his potential links to the force itself, including at least one policeman who we believe acts as an informant to him and is a current serving detective sergeant. We were unsure who we could trust with our findings but when Steve met you both the other night at Mere, we thought it was a perfect opportunity, especially as Wade's is involved, although unbeknownst to you Bill, I am sure," John added quickly before Bill could protest.

Bill gave John a quizzical look and said, "I am sure you will explain your suspicions but as I said on the phone, I am confident you are mistaken about my company's involvement in anything illegal, hence my invitation to Leo to join us. I am sure we can clear everything up. I presume this has something to do with the disappearance of one of our drivers down here a couple of years ago. Leo was kind enough to do a little research when Steve introduced you into our conversation, John, and he discovered your link to that case, which is still open I believe."

"Yes, that was indeed the starting point in all this, but it was only the catalyst which set us off on the investigation. It is best if I walk you through everything we have found out so far – there are some solid facts plus a lot of circumstantial evidence and coincidences, but when they are all combined, we believe they make a strong case against two people and their illicit business organisation."

"May I ask who these two people are?" asked the Chief Constable.

"Jonathan Underwood and Emrys Williams, Wade's solicitor and accountant," John announced.

"Why am I not surprised?" said Bill quietly, almost to himself.

"But again Bill, we don't think your company is directly involved. But we do think Underwood is using people within your firm."

"Okay," the ex-owner of Wade Manufacturing conceded, "let's hear what you have found out."

"Right, I'll start with the solicitor, Underwood, who we believe to be the man running the whole thing. He was with the Public Defender's Service in Swansea for over ten years before setting up his own practice in Manchester so he had plenty of opportunity to make a significant number of contacts within the criminal fraternity. He is not in general practice as far as we know but appears to just work for a small number of businesses, all apparently legal and above board, Wade's being one of them. In every case, it appears that he has approached the firms directly with an offer of cash from an offshore investment company and part of the deal always involves him being appointed their company solicitor and Williams & Co being appointed their new company accountants.

"Emrys Williams, who heads up the accountancy firm,

also has his roots in South Wales. He originally worked for a large firm of accountants in Cardiff before two partners were arrested and convicted of money laundering, fraud and embezzlement, although he was not accused of anything himself – bit of a coincidence don't you think? He left the company and, shortly after gaining all his accountancy qualifications at another Cardiff firm, set up his own business. This just happened to coincide with Underwood moving up to Manchester to set up his own practice.

"The first firms they were involved with as far as we know were Boston Heating and Ventilating Supplies in Hull and McConnell Transport and Warehousing in Liverpool. Both are legitimately trading companies but we believe Peter Boston also imports drugs from Amsterdam via the Rotterdam to Hull ferry and McConnell distributes them to a dealer network throughout the country. With regard to Wade's, obviously Bill knows of Underwood's and Williams' involvement with them but we also believe they use the house here in Moelfre as a drop point for the smuggling of precious gemstones from Nigeria. The Wade's delivery driver who goes back and forth to their Dublin shop brings the stones into the Manchester warehouse and passes them on, via John Bootle, we believe, to Brian Mather who then delivers them to Underwood. What happens to them then we don't know. We have not actually seen the gemstones but we have seen, once a month in the middle of the night, two men leave a ship anchored in the bay by a small, powered dinghy and deliver a package to the cottage and then return to their ship.

The package is a cylindrical tube about nine inches long and four inches in diameter. The ship is the *MV Caracas* which sails between Lagos and Liverpool once a month."

John paused and looked at his two guests for their reactions.

"Well you have certainly both been very busy, and I would be very interested in learning how you found all this out later. But I presume you have more information? Although, as you said, when you put all these pieces together it certainly looks very damning in itself," observed Leo. "What do you think about the smuggling and Brian Mather's involvement Bill?"

"What, that my daughter has married a criminal who is involved with our company solicitor and accountant in diamond smuggling? Initial reaction – absolutely incredible, unbelievable. But on reflection, I suppose I am not totally surprised that something illegal is going on. I have always been somewhat suspicious of our Mr Underwood and his offshore investment company – but who questions a solicitor, especially one with his credentials, and an apparently well-established, respectable accountancy firm? They made us an offer my daughter and her husband apparently couldn't refuse, as the famous line goes, at a time when we were struggling. By the way, to add to your coincidences, Brian Mather comes from Swansea and I believe had a somewhat shady background although I don't know of anything specific. Also, for your further information, the board has recently passed an additional expansion project for Wade's with a projected cost of just over £2million, again to be financed through Underwood's offshore investment company," the bemused ex-director added.

"It would appear that Mr Underwood's organisation is proving very profitable," agreed the Chief Constable. "What else do you have John?" Leo continued.

"As I mentioned, we believe Underwood has connections in the force, one of which I am pretty sure of but have no concrete evidence I must admit. He was my detective sergeant before I left the police last year and he was the main investigative officer in the Wade's missing driver case. Again, he originated in Swansea, transferred to Manchester shortly after Underwood set up shop in Manchester and then moved over to North Wales, I presume when they started the smuggling business in order to keep an eye on things over here. We still don't know what happened to that driver but now we know about his probable smuggling involvement it would explain why the detective sergeant didn't appear to dig too deeply into it and was happy to pass it off as a simple 'missing persons' case. Mr Underwood is obviously very well organised and also probably very well connected which is why we are cautious as to who we contact with this information. We have no idea how many other policemen he has on his payroll."

"Yes I see," agreed the Chief Constable. "And how did you find out all this as a matter of interest?"

"It's a long story Leo, over several months. We had help with Boston's over in Hull — one of my ex-colleagues put me in touch with a retired detective over there who we were convinced we could trust and he did all the work relating to them. I also got in touch with a private investigator I have passed work to in the past and he dug into Underwood's history and the companies the solicitor is involved with, at least the ones he could find out about. And by way of another coincidence, all the firms Underwood represents, and there are six of them we know about, are sited or have offices close to ferry terminal ports and have transport facilities of one kind or another. We have only looked at Boston's and Wade's so far but I would not be surprised if one or more of the others are also involved in some form of illicit dealings, if only as part of the drug dealership network or laundering the drug money."

"How does all this affect us Leo?" the Non-Executive Director of Wade's asked anxiously.

"Good question Bill," his friend replied. "If everything that John and Steve have uncovered turns out to be true, and I have no reason to doubt their conclusions, it is going to be a mess old friend. Wade's as a company, and you and Joanna specifically, should be in the clear, but the potential financial ramifications to your business are a different matter. From what John is saying, your company may have received large amounts of funding from an illegal source, albeit unwittingly in your case, which is obviously a serious matter, but other people will have to sort that out later if it is all proven. The fact you were obviously in the dark about it all will help, as will the fact that you are part of the discovery and potential prosecution so to speak. What are you proposing John?"

"Actually, we were hoping that after hearing our story, you would be able to suggest a course of action Leo," John replied tentatively.

There was silence for a short time and then finally the Chief Constable spoke. "I think you have made a very good case, albeit a little light on actual facts or concrete evidence. But as you said, when you put it all together, your conclusions are probably correct. As you also suggested, we need to be careful about who we involve. Tomorrow when I am back in the office, I will have a quiet chat with my number two, Chief Superintendent Jonny Radcliffe, and run it by him. I think we will probably have to involve a couple of other forces and put together an independent task force under Jonny's leadership, thus hopefully reducing the chance of tipping off any allies of our Mr Underwood. Bill, you will have to carry on as normal I'm afraid – we don't want to alert Mather, if indeed he is involved," Leo concluded, looking around at the three other men expectantly in case they wanted to add anything.

"That sounds like a plan Leo," agreed John, "we will leave everything to you. We will be available to join in any meetings or take any calls from whoever is part of the investigation if anyone needs to speak to us of course. Thanks again to both of you for coming down – it will certainly take a load off our minds now that we know there will be an official investigation and we can leave it in your hands," John said finally.

"Yes, thanks, I will definitely sleep better now," echoed Steve. "Have you made any plans for lunch?" he asked, looking at his watch. "We can recommend our local pub, they do excellent lunches both cooked and sandwiches and the view over the bay is fabulous."

"Sounds perfect," Leo replied. "What do you say Bill, a bite to eat before we drive back?"

"Definitely," agreed his friend. "Would you two like to join us?" Bill asked.

"No thanks," John replied. "It will give you chance to talk over what we have discussed, so probably better if we don't."

"Alright, if you are sure we will say cheerio and keep in touch," Leo concluded.

With that, Steve passed them a note with his and John's mobile and email information, gave them directions to the nearby pub and then waved them off at the door.

"Well I think that went well Steve, don't you?" John asked.

"Yes, agreed," Steve replied. "I think I will be off as well and get some lunch myself. See you at the pub tomorrow night as usual?"

"Definitely," said John with a relieved smile.

PART FOUR

Chapter 23

Three days after his meeting in Moelfre with Steve Guest and retired Detective Chief Inspector John Wyn Thomas, Leonard Bright was at his desk reading the report that John had agreed to put together and had sent to his personal email address the previous evening. The report contained all the information John and Steve had gathered, together with their inferences and conclusions. After reading the report for a second time, the Chief Constable rang through to his personal secretary.

"Pam, please can you call Chief Superintendent Radcliffe and ask him to come and see me at his earliest convenience."

"Yes Sir, will do," she replied and almost immediately called him back. "He is in a meeting Sir. I have left him a message."

"Thanks Pam," the Chief Constable replied.

His secretary called back twenty minutes later.

"The Chief Superintendent has just come out of the meeting Sir and says he can pop over at about 4pm if that is convenient."

"Yes that would be fine Pam, tell him I will see him then."

At 3.55pm prompt, Pam called through to the Chief

Constable. "Chief Superintendent Radcliffe is here to see you Sir."

"Thanks Pam, ask him to come through please."

There was a knock on Leonard's door and his number two entered and stepped forward to shake the Chief Constable's hand as he stood up from behind his desk.

"Afternoon Sir. I trust you are well?"

"Yes fine thanks, Jonny, and you?" replied the Chief Constable. "Sit down please."

"What can I do for you, Sir?" the Chief Superintendent asked as he sat down in one of the chairs opposite the Chief Constable.

"I have received some information through a private source which, if confirmed, could lead to some serious charges being brought against what is potentially a large criminal organisation," replied Leo as he passed over the file which John Wyn Thomas had sent him earlier.

"You are only the second person to see this, apart from the man who wrote it of course, who is a recently retired Detective Chief Inspector so you can take it that the allegations should be taken very seriously. Take some time to read it and then we can discuss our plan of action. Would you like a drink?" Leonard asked.

"Coffee please Sir, white no sugar," Jonny replied as he opened the file and began reading.

The Chief Constable buzzed through to his secretary on the intercom. "Pam, please could we have two coffees, both white, one with no sugar and my usual sweetener for me."

"No problem Sir," Leonard's secretary replied and went through to the small kitchen and returned with the two coffees as ordered and took them through to the two senior police officers.

"Thanks very much Pam," Leonard said as she placed the two cups on coasters on his desk beside the two policemen.

They sat in silence as Jonny read the report for a second time and they drank their coffee.

On completing his second read through, and after sitting quietly for a further few minutes, the Chief Superintendent finally broke the silence.

"Quite a story Sir. Have you met the author?"

"Yes, I went down to Moelfre at Bill Wade's invitation and met up with both retired DCI John Wyn Thomas and Steve Guest, where I heard all this for the first time. There is no doubt that they have put a lot of time and effort into their investigation and they totally believe everything they say in that report."

"It certainly suggests there is a strong possibility of some serious criminal activity Sir, but there is no hard evidence linking Underwood and Williams directly to anything," concluded the Chief Superintendent. "How do you want to proceed?"

"I agree but obviously if there is police involvement, and they are pretty sure at least one officer is implicated and goodness knows how many more may be, then we will have to tread very cautiously if we don't want to tip our hand. Initially, what we need to do is confirm that what they are accusing Underwood of is in fact true and provide positive proof of the drug trade and gemstone smuggling and whatever else we find he is involved with. Once we have that, we can then decide our next step, either a co-ordinated official investigation by the local forces or pass it over to Serious Crimes if we think that is the best option.

"My suggestion Jonny is that we instigate two completely separate investigations, one into Boston's and the drugs in Hull and the other into Wade's and the gemstone smuggling on Anglesey, saying they are based on tip-offs we have received locally but initially only we will know they are connected. I suggest you co-ordinate both investigations using different forces from other areas to minimise the chance of potentially alerting Underwood or anyone who might be involved with him. In fact, you need to do a background check on any officer you involve in the investigation to try and ensure they have no links to Underwood, Williams or Swansea if possible. I suggest you use officers from Northumbria for the Hull investigation and perhaps Cumbria for Anglesey and Wade's. I know the Chief Constables of both forces personally and will help if needed with any necessary personnel checks or authorisations. I think that is about everything for the moment. Any thoughts or questions?" the Chief Constable concluded.

"Not for the moment Sir, I'll give it some thought and get back to you. Can I take the file?"

"Of course, let me know anything you need."

With that, the Chief Superintendent stood up and left.

The following Wednesday, he was back in his boss's office.

"The two teams are set up and will start their investigations next week Sir," Jonny reported. "I have detailed the Hull team initially to follow the delivery vehicles to and from Boston's to find the point of origin of the truck delivering the suspected drugs from Europe and confirm the involvement of McConnell's in the UK distribution. According to the report, they happen weekly so we should get some confirmation pretty quickly. The Anglesey operation is a lot more involved – as it only apparently happens once a month, it will take more time to investigate and confirm. I stressed the importance to each team of treating everything they do and find in the strictest confidence and reporting only to me. This was confirmed to them by their senior officers – thank you for arranging that for me."

"No problem, Jonny. Let's hope this bears fruit. Anything else?"

"No Sir, that about covers it for now. I will update you as soon as I get any feedback from either team."

With that, he left the Chief Constable's office and the official investigation into Jonathon T Underwood's illegal organisation was under way.

Chapter 24

The team from the Northumbria police force investigating Boston's potential links to the drugs trade consisted of a detective sergeant, a detective constable plus two constables from their traffic division to act as drivers for the two unmarked police cars that they would be using to track the drugs into the country and their subsequent distribution.

Using the information that the Cheshire-based Chief Superintendent had provided, the two cars were in position early on the Thursday morning. One was near the Boston Heating and Ventilation Supplies premises on the Dairycoates Industrial Estate. At just after 7am, as anticipated, the white Luton van left Boston's yard and drove to the P&O Ferry terminal at Hull in time to catch the 9am ferry to Rotterdam with one unmarked police car following discreetly behind. The second police car was already parked near the front of the queue ready to board the ferry once the departure of the Luton and his colleague from Boston's had been confirmed.

All three vehicles boarded the ferry successfully and the twelve-hour crossing was uneventful, allowing the four undercover policemen plenty of opportunities to take some excellent photographs of the driver and his Luton van during the voyage. On arrival at Rotterdam, the two unmarked police cars, which both left the ferry before the Luton van, were able to take up good positions behind it as it left the port and set off down the A13 before joining the A4 for the seventy-minute journey to Amsterdam. Shortly after passing Schiphol Airport, they turned off the A4 onto the A10 and then about half a mile later turned off left into a large industrial estate. The two unmarked cars followed at a discreet distance and saw the Luton turn into the gateway to a small, unmarked warehouse property which was surrounded by a high chain-linked fence and park outside the closed doors. The driver got out of the van and locked the door and was immediately met by a man leaving the warehouse through a small door at the side of the main entrance. The two men then got into a black Volvo estate and drove off through the main gate towards the city centre. The policemen made a note of the warehouse's location and then drove back to their pre-booked hotel by the airport, ready to return early the following morning to monitor the next stage of the Luton's journey.

The two unmarked police cars were in position at 8am. They knew nothing was probably going to happen too early in the day as they presumed the Luton would be returning to Hull on the 5pm ferry but they wanted to observe the activity at the warehouse for future reference. This included taking as many photographs as possible of the various people and vehicles which came and went to the industrial unit throughout the day.

The Luton driver returned just after 11am, driven back in the black Volvo estate. He disappeared into the warehouse with his driver and appeared about thirty minutes later through the main warehouse doors, went to the Luton, unlocked the cab and lowered the back tail-lift. At the same time, two men began bringing several large boxes and crates out of the building and placing them behind the van. They then placed them onto the tail-lift and began loading them into the back of the white Luton. The police officers were able to get a number of very good shots of the loading and of all the people involved. Once the boxes and crates were all on board, the van driver locked up the Luton and went back inside the warehouse. He reappeared just after 2pm, got into his van and drove it out through the main gates and headed back towards Rotterdam with the two unmarked police cars in tow. The three vehicles all boarded the 5pm ferry back to Hull and arrived in the port after a smooth crossing at just after 4.30 on the Saturday morning. The driver headed straight to Boston's where he was let into the yard by Peter Boston himself. He drove the van straight into the open main warehouse, locked the vehicle, came out of the warehouse, which Boston locked after him, and left in his own black Audi A4 estate, followed by Boston's Range Rover Discovery, Boston closing and locking the main gate on their departure.

According to their notes, the policemen knew that nothing would happen till later on in the day so they decided to park up nearby and catch a few hours' sleep before being back in position for around 9am.

They were actually in place by 8.30am after filling up with diesel at a local petrol station. Sure enough, just after 9.30am,

Peter Boston and the Luton van driver arrived almost together in their respective private vehicles. Peter opened the yard and waved the Audi through, following him through himself and leaving the gates open. He opened the main roller doors to the warehouse and the van driver reversed the Luton back through the open doors. The two men unloaded the boxes and crates from the back of the van and then sat down on a crate each, having a cigarette and chatting while the detectives, at a safe distance and well concealed from their view, snapped merrily away, capturing everything that happened on film.

Then came the first change to the predicted itinerary. Instead of two white Transit vans bearing the McConnell Transport & Warehousing lettering on the side, two white Mercedes-Benz Sprinter vans with no logo appeared, closely followed by one of Boston's own Citroen vans complete with their own company logo. The vehicles drove into the yard and parked beside the Luton van and the unloaded boxes. The drivers got out and helped the Luton driver load up three boxes which Peter Boston indicated into each of the two Sprinters and one into the Citroen.

As they were loading up the vans, the Detective Sergeant called his colleague in the second car.

"This wasn't in the script – there's only supposed to be two McConnell vans, one going local and one to Liverpool."

"That's right, Sarge, what do you think?" the Detective Constable replied.

"We'll leave the Citroen which will probably be doing the

local run. We'll follow the two Sprinters. If they split up, you take the '67' plate and I'll take the '68' okay?"

"Will do," his colleague replied.

As soon as the two Sprinters were loaded, they left the yard and headed out on the A63 towards the M62 motorway going west with the two unmarked police cars following behind.

"Perhaps they're new additions to their fleet and McConnell's have just not had these vans painted yet," the Detective Sergeant suggested when he called his colleague back as they both drove up the slip road to join the M62 to Leeds, Manchester and Liverpool, "and they have an additional drop-off point so they need two vehicles."

"Could be," the Detective Constable replied. "Good job we filled up both cars earlier at that petrol station."

"True," his partner agreed and ended the call.

The second change came shortly afterwards when instead of continuing along the M62 the two Sprinters signalled left off the motorway at the M18 intersection and joined that motorway going south.

The two unmarked police cars followed the vans and joined the M18.

"Well it appears we're not going to Liverpool, whether they're McConnell vans are not, looks like we are headed for the M1 and all points south," the Detective Sergeant observed to his colleagues in the second car. "Let's not lose them."

The Detective Sergeant's guess proved correct as the M18 merged into the M1 and they all headed towards the south.

The third change came when the two vans split up as one of them, the '67' plate, signalled to exit the M1 at Junction 24 and the other one carried on south towards London.

"That's your van leaving," the Detective Sergeant said when he called the second car. "I'll follow '68' on the M1. Keep in touch."

"Will do," his colleague replied.

Ten minutes later, the Detective Constable called him back. "We are on the M42 going towards Birmingham boss."

"Okay, see where he goes and if he offloads the cases. We're still on the M1. I have a feeling we're on our way to London. Speak to you when we arrive at wherever we are going." With that, he settled in for the rest of the journey.

His destination turned out to be Cranborne Industrial Estate at Potters Bar just off the A1M and close to the M25. They followed the van onto the estate and saw it pull into the yard of a small industrial unit which had an office built on to a small warehouse. There was no company name or signage on the gated entrance that they could see. The unmarked police car drove past the fenced entrance and stopped about 100 yards farther along the road behind a large articulated lorry which was parked up. The Detective Sergeant took out his camera with the telephoto lens and had a clear view of the Sprinter van. He saw the driver get out and be joined immediately by someone who came out of the front office door and opened the warehouse roller door. The driver opened the back of the van and the two men carried the three boxes into the warehouse, disappearing from view. Ten minutes later, the driver reappeared, locked the van doors and went into the office. Having photographed as much as he could, and made a note of the site's position in the estate on a small map he drew in his notebook, the detective spoke to his driver. "That's about all we can do for today, let's head back home. We can stop at the services for a bite to eat and to freshen up. It's been a long day but very fruitful I think. Hopefully DC Sweeney will have had an equally successful one."

The driver started up the car and headed back to the north.

During the journey home, the Detective Sergeant's mobile rang. "Evening Jim, how did it go?" he asked.

"Very well. We followed them to a small industrial estate just off the M6 toll road at Sutton Coldfield and they took the three cases into a small warehouse there. We're on our way home, I'll send you a full report later when we get back. Where did you end up?"

"An industrial estate just outside Potters Bar close to the M25 and M1 junction," the Detective Sergeant replied.

"What's happening tomorrow?" the DC asked.

"Rest up at the hotel tonight and see what they want us to do next. It's been a long day but very successful I think. Once I receive your report I'll put it together with mine and forward them both onto the Chief Super. After that, we will have to wait and see. Have a safe journey and I'll see you later."

The Detective Sergeant ended the call and settled back for the long journey home.

Chapter 25

While the Northumbria team were crossing the North Sea on their way to Rotterdam, the Cumbria Police Force team were checking into their six-bedroom, four-bathroom holiday let just outside Benllech on Anglesey. The house had been booked for four weeks as the object of their investigation, the *MV Caracas*, was not due to arrive in the waters around Moelfre for another two weeks. This gave the team plenty of time to survey the area surrounding the bungalow for the best spots to observe any potential drop-offs without themselves being seen either from the bungalow or by the people arriving on the shore. In their briefing with Chief Superintendent Radcliffe, it had not been specified what the contents of the package might be, just that someone from the *Caracas* would come ashore sometime between midnight and 6am and leave it outside the back door of Plas Meirion before returning to the ship. They were to take as many shots of the incoming seamen, package drop and its retrieval by the man in the house as possible using their high-powered camera and telephoto lens which was fitted with a special lens for night vision. They were then to follow the occupant of the house into Manchester the following day, confirming his ETA at Wade's with the Chief Superintendent as they were nearing the outskirts of the City.

They knew the bungalow occupant's movements each week as he kept to a regular schedule of trips between home, Manchester and Wade's large retail shop in Dublin and as Plas Meirion backed onto the Anglesey Coastal Path, which was popular with both local walkers and serious hikers, they were able to survey the area with very little chance of arousing any suspicion.

The *MV Caracas* anchored in the bay between Lligwy and Moelfre two weeks later on the Monday afternoon as expected. The four policemen took up their positions just before 11pm on the Tuesday, two together on each side of the bungalow over a hundred metres away. They were each midway between Plas Meirion and the narrow path which led from the shore to the back of the house, slightly above and in perfect positions to take photographs of everything that might happen with no chance of being spotted by the seamen or the Wade's driver.

At 2.15am, shortly after the police officers heard the muffled sound of a small outboard motor, a figure emerged from the shore below onto the narrow pathway at the rear of the bungalow, walked carefully up to the back door and placed what looked like a short black cylinder on the doorstep. The man then rang the doorbell, looked furtively around and quickly retraced his steps back down the path and disappeared towards the shore. Shortly afterwards, the policemen heard the muffled engine sound again and then it slowly disappeared. Five minutes later, the bungalow occupant appeared at the back door, retrieved the package and went back inside. A few minutes later, the lights in the house went out and everything was quiet. The policemen waited fifteen minutes and then carefully returned to their two cars which were parked out of sight about a quarter of a mile away and headed back to their rented house in Benllech.

The Detective Inspector heading up the team texted Chief Superintendent Radcliffe on the journey back to the house with the simple message, "Mission accomplished. Will follow suspect to Manchester tomorrow."

The two cars were in position at 8.30 the next morning, one on the road just outside Moelfre and the second in Benllech. As the Wade's Transit van passed the first car at Moelfre, the Detective Sergeant called his colleague. "He's on his way, should be with you in about five minutes." He then waited a couple of minutes and followed on.

The two unmarked police cars followed the Transit, regularly changing positions to avoid any chance of being spotted by the Transit driver.

Just as the van was nearing the end of the M56, the Detective Inspector called Radcliffe as arranged. "He should be arriving at Wade's in about fifteen or twenty minutes Sir."

"Thank you Frank, good work. We will take it from here. Have a safe journey home and I look forward to receiving your report."

"Thank you Sir, it will be with you by tomorrow lunchtime," the DI replied before calling his colleagues in the second car. "Okay Phil, we're done. Head back home and I'll see you at 9am tomorrow at the office."

With that, the two cars turned off the M56 and joined the M60 westbound before turning onto the M61, feeding onto the M6 northbound and heading home.

On receiving the call from the Detective Inspector who had been following the Wade's van, Jonny Radcliffe called William Wade as arranged.

William had gone into the office that Wednesday morning on the pretext of talking to Brian Mather about the proposed expansion plans. William had asked Brian when he was free that day and Brian had explained that he would be at their solicitors from 2pm and had suggested William drop in any time during the morning.

"He will be with you in about fifteen or twenty minutes, William," the Chief Superintendent said. "Let me know what happens."

"Will do," William replied and ended the call. Ten minutes later, he wandered down to where the vans were loaded and unloaded at the entrance to the main warehouse. He got himself a coffee from the free vending machine and struck up a conversation with one of the warehousemen who was standing near the open roller doors.

Shortly afterwards, the white Transit driven by Mat Dawson came to a stop just inside the building. As Mat stepped out of the vehicle, John Bootle came down the stairs into the unloading bay from his office and went over to him.

"Everything okay, Mat?" the Transport Manager asked.

"Yes fine thanks, Mr Bootle. I have a few returns from Dublin," Mat replied.

"No problem, unload them and check them in to stores and then I'll see you in my office."

"Will do," Mat confirmed and then opened the rear doors of the Transit and started taking the returned stock out and walking over to the stores counter at the rear of the warehouse. When he finished, he closed the doors, went round to the passenger door, reached in and retrieved his backpack form the seat. He then walked up the stairs to the Transport Manager's office, knocked on the door and went in, closing the door behind him.

As he did, William finished his conversation and followed Mat up into the office area, walking past John Bootle's office and into his own just across the open plan administration area. He left the door ajar and had a good view of the Transport Manager's door. Ten minutes later, Mat reappeared carrying his backpack and returned to the warehouse. After loading up the new stock for the Dublin store, he had a coffee from the vending machine before getting back into the Transit, driving out of the yard and returning to Anglesey.

Shortly after Mat left the Transport Manager's office, William saw John Bootle appear carrying another black backpack, walk past the boardroom and knock twice on Brian Mather's office door before entering. He reappeared almost immediately but without the backpack. As the Transport Manager left to return to his own office, William stood up and walked over to Brian's office before knocking, opening the door and going in, just in time to see him zipping up the black backpack and putting it down on the floor next to his desk.

"Is this a good time?" William asked. "Sorry, it's a bit later than I planned but I got tied up down in the warehouse."

"Not really, Bill," Brian replied. "I'm just about to go and get a bite to eat before my two o'clock appointment at the solicitors. Is it important or can it wait?"

"No problem Brian, it can wait. I just wanted to ask you about that transport company you're recommending for the online delivery service. I'll give you a call and we'll rearrange." With that, William went back to his own office, again leaving the door ajar, and busied himself shuffling some paperwork around.

About fifteen minutes later, Brian Mather came out of his office with the black backpack over his shoulder, went down to the car park at the rear of the building, got in his car and drove out towards Manchester.

William stood, went to his office door, closed it and took out his mobile phone. He searched for the newly added contact number and pressed call. "Mather has just left carrying a black backpack on the way to his 2pm appointment with Underwood in Manchester," he said when the call was answered.

"Thanks, William," replied Chief Superintendent Radcliffe who was sitting in his car which was parked in the multi-storey car park just behind Piccadilly Station. "Did you see anything of significance this morning?"

"Not really. I managed to get into the warehouse when the Transit arrived. After unloading some stock, the driver went into John Bootle's office carrying his backpack and came out shortly afterwards still carrying it. I couldn't see if he had taken anything out of it and left it with John though. John then went into Brian's office carrying a different backpack and came out again almost immediately without it. A short time afterwards, Brian came out of his office carrying that same backpack and left in his car."

"Excellent William. Thanks again for your help," replied Radcliffe before ending the call.

As no one at Wade's or Underwood's knew the Chief Superintendent, he had volunteered to sit in the bistro across from the solicitor's office and watch for any potential developments after Mather's meeting with Underwood and to follow either party if he deemed it necessary and if safe to do so without jeopardising the operation.

At 1.15pm, he left his car and walked across what used to be Piccadilly Gardens before it was transformed into a concrete wasteland and bus and Metrolink interchange, down Fountain Street, left into York Street and then right into West Mosely Street. He walked just past the entrance to the offices which housed the solicitor's practice and immediately crossed the road and entered the bistro which directly faced them. At 1.35pm, he sat down at one of the window tables, took out a laptop from his leather briefcase and a pad and paper. He opened the laptop and turned it on and appeared to start working, just like three other people who were doing exactly the same at three other tables. Almost immediately, a smartly dressed waiter appeared holding a menu.

"Will you be eating with us today sir?" he asked politely

and offered the menu which the Chief Superintendent accepted.

After briefly scanning what was on offer, he replied, "I'll have the chilli con carne with a side salad and a glass of the pinot grigio please."

"Thank you sir," the waiter said, and the Chief Superintendent went back to his laptop while keeping an eye on the office entrance across the road.

At 1.55pm, he saw Brian Mather walking up West Mosely Street towards the solicitor's building carrying the black backpack; he entered the office building through the revolving doors and walked over to the reception desk. After briefly chatting to the receptionist, he walked towards the lifts and disappeared into the left-hand one.

Thirty-five minutes later, Brian reappeared still carrying the backpack and walked back up the street towards Piccadilly Gardens.

Five minutes after the Operations Director left the building, Underwood's personal iPhone pinged informing him that he had an incoming text message. He picked up the phone, punched in his PIN to access the menu, pressed the 'message' icon and opened the message: "Do not take the package to Oxford Road. You are being watched. Stay in your office until at least 4pm and then leave. Do not carry anything out with you and go straight home. You can deal with the package safely tomorrow. If your wife is not at home, make some calls from your office mobile as soon as you arrive to establish your presence there. Phone this number tonight between 7-8pm on a secure line. I can help. A friend."

The blood drained from the solicitor's face as the significance of the message and its possible ramifications slowly sunk in. Not only did the sender appear to know about Wade's and his smuggling operations but he or she also seemed to know that he was involved with the jewellery shop on Oxford Road. 'Watched by whom?' he wondered. He was certain it couldn't be the police or he would have heard about it through his contacts. He felt as if his whole business operation was crumbling in front of him as he stared disbelievingly at the screen. 'Stay calm,' he told himself, 'there's nothing you can do now. Phone the number tonight and see what he or she wants and how much it is going to cost.'

He called through to his secretary. "Tricia, I'm not going out to my afternoon appointment after all, they've just cancelled. I have a few things to finish up here and then I'll be off home."

"Alright, Mr Underwood. Will you be in tomorrow?" she asked.

"Yes, about 10am," he confirmed. He tried to go back to a supply contract he was drawing up for Wade's new online catalogue provision to distract him from the text he had just received which he knew would undoubtedly change his life and probably not for the better.

Across the road in the bistro, the Chief Superintendent had finished his meal and ordered a coffee. At 3.45pm, and on his second coffee, he called William Wade on his mobile.

"Afternoon Bill, can you speak?"

"Yes," he replied. "I'm at home and my wife is out with some friends shopping."

"Can you ring your solicitor's office and ask to speak to Underwood? It's over an hour since Mather left and I'd like to check that he is still there and hasn't slipped out of a back door or something. Just ask him when he is next at your place because you would like to have a chat with him about the expansion, the same storyline you put to Brian."

"Okay, will do and I'll give you a call back." William hung up and called the solicitor's office. Having announced who he was to the lady who answered and saying that he would like to speak to Mr Underwood, he was put through to Jonathon.

"Afternoon Bill, what can I do for you?" the solicitor asked.

"Afternoon Jonathon. Sorry for interrupting but when are you next over at Trafford Park? I would like to have a chat with you about this expansion project."

"Yes, Brian mentioned at our meeting earlier that you were looking to speak to him about it as well. I'm just wrapping things up here and am about to leave and head home. I'll give you a call tomorrow and we can fix something up. Is that okay with you?" Jonathon asked.

"Yes, that's fine, speak to you tomorrow then." Bill ended the call and rang the Chief Superintendent straight back.

"I have just spoken to him at his office and he said he was about to leave and go home."

"Excellent, Bill. Thank you very much for all your help today. I'll keep in touch."

Five minutes later, the solicitor appeared at the entrance to the offices, stepped out of the revolving doors onto the pavement, paused as though deciding which way to go and then headed down the road towards the private car park where his BMW was parked. As he stood outside the doorway, the Chief Superintendent got a perfect shot of him leaving on his phone's camera from inside the bistro timed at 4.13pm and not carrying any kind of carrycase or parcel. Once the solicitor was out of sight, he called over the waiter and paid the bill, giving him a very generous tip. He then packed away his laptop, the pad with his newly formed action plan and pen and left the bistro, heading back to his car in the Piccadilly Station car park.

Chapter 26

Jonathon arrived home at just after 5.30pm to be met by his wife.

"You're home early this evening darling, everything alright?" she asked.

"Yes fine thanks. I had an afternoon appointment cancelled so I came on home. Had a good day?" he asked cheerily.

"Yes, I've been over at Lucy's," Abigail replied. "Anything special you'd like for dinner?"

"How do you fancy going out somewhere?" he answered. "I'll have a shower and then there are a couple of things I need to do for work. We could go out about eight, what do you think?" he suggested.

"Sounds lovely Jonathon, we could go to Luigi's. We've not been for a while. I can wear that new outfit I bought in town yesterday," she agreed happily.

"Excellent, I'll go for my shower then," said Jonathon and disappeared up to their bedroom.

After showering, Jonathon spent about thirty minutes with his wife chatting about her day before excusing himself just before 7pm and going into the study which served as his home office. He closed the door while his wife went back upstairs to take out her new outfit and get ready for their outing to her favourite Italian restaurant.

At 7.15pm, he took out an unused PAYG phone from the top drawer and called the number of the phone which had sent him the earth-shattering text earlier in the day. He had agonised over whether to call his partner Emrys Williams to warn him of their potentially impending danger but had decided against it until he had spoken to the caller in order to fully assess their precarious predicament.

The call was answered after just three rings.

"Good evening Jonathon, so pleased you returned my call," came the cheery reply. "Hopefully I can help resolve the very unfortunate situation you find yourself in."

Jonathon breathed a sigh of relief. The voice was obviously that of a well-educated, mature man with a calm demeanour – someone he could work with he thought hopefully.

"I am sure you were shocked and somewhat taken aback by my message and will obviously be suspicious of my motives. The purpose of this initial chat is for me to explain a little about myself, suggest a possible way out of your dilemma and assure you I have your best interests at heart."

"That is reassuring," Jonathon replied evenly. "You have my full attention."

"Excellent, firstly a little about myself and my line of work," the voice on the other phone continued as he referred to one of the two manilla files he had retrieved earlier from the bottom drawer of a three-drawer filing cabinet next to his desk. Each drawer had a reference card showing its contents, the top one A to H, the second one I to P and the bottom drawer Q to

Z. "You will be surprised to learn that I have been following your career for a couple of years now, since you set up your new practice in Manchester after all those successful years with the Public Defenders Service and your subsequent partnership with Emrys Williams. By the way, much of the information we unearthed about your organisation came from investigating your Welsh accountant," he said as he glanced at the second folder on his desk. "For someone who relies so much on the internet for your clandestine dealings, his electronic security systems are quite basic my colleague informs me."

Jonathon sat stunned, looking out through his study window as these new revelations hit home.

"You were first brought to my attention," the mysterious caller continued smoothly, "over that business with the disappearance of the Wade's delivery driver which obviously was a lot more involved than a simple missing persons case. You see, I am a collector of information, specifically that which involves criminals and their illegal activities, and that has the potential to be used profitably by both parties, although in different ways. It was obvious to me after fortuitously coming across the incident that it and its participants merited more investigation, which of course led me to uncover your gemstone smuggling operation. Let me reassure you immediately Jonathon that I am not a blackmailer – in fact, quite the opposite. I use the intelligence I have gathered over time to help criminals avoid any potentially serious charges which may be brought against them. Then, to recompense myself for my time, energy and the resources I have used, I charge my client or clients what I believe to be a fair market rate in order to preserve their freedom or avoid any potentially large fines and resulting legal costs."

The voice paused to let this totally unexpected declaration sink in with Jonathon and then, when the solicitor refrained from commenting, he continued. "I have a background in computing and IT which I put to good effect in my intelligence gathering. I also employ a man who I believe is one of the best computer and system hackers around, combined with a network of informers which I have built up over the years. I'm a bit of a romantic I know but I see myself as the antithesis of one of my fictional boyhood heroes, Sherlock Holmes, who used his skills and vast knowledge of all things criminal for the good of society. Then again, I certainly do not see myself as a Moriarty figure who was after all a criminal, something I certainly consider myself not to be, but I digress," the man continued. "Yes, it didn't take long once I started to look at Wade's and their business to discover your and Mr William's involvement with them and then, with the help of my accomplished hacker, we soon unearthed your various business partnerships and dealings, both illegal and legal, and your clandestine offshore banking arrangements and shell companies posing as your mysterious 'company investors'."

"If you are so well informed about my businesses, why did you not come to me before in order to collect payment?" Jonathon asked.

"As I said, I am not a blackmailer Jonathon. I only approach prospective clients if I believe they are in need of my unique services. If you had gone through life completely undetected by the criminal justice agencies then you would never have heard from me. I repeat, I am here to help at a time of need."

"Forgive my scepticism but it is all a little hard to believe," the solicitor replied.

"I understand, which is why I said at the start of the call that this is a preliminary introduction to myself and the services I offer. I think the little I have disclosed to you so far has shown I have a thorough understanding of your organisation although I have only mentioned Wade's, the gemstone smuggling and the offshore banking arrangement links so far. I feel we can take it as read that I know all about the drugs, the art gallery and the auction house – do you agree?"

"What are you proposing?" Jonathon asked, not wishing to confirm any of the mysterious caller's professed knowledge and still very much in shock at all the information he had gathered concerning his businesses, both legal and illegal.

"As I warned you in the text message, you are under investigation by the police. How I know, we will leave for the moment but you can be certain that it is so. Your local 'eyes and ears' is unaware of it because Charlie's involvement with you is already suspected so they have brought people in from outside forces. I am informed that so far they have only uncovered the drug importation business from Amsterdam through Boston's and its subsequent distribution down to the industrial sites at Potters Bar and Sutton Coldfield and the gemstone smuggling operation from Nigeria via the *Caracas*, Anglesey and Wade's."

The voice paused again, waiting for a reaction from the solicitor, but again Jonathon remained silent, taking in the staggering new realisation that what he believed to be two well-run clandestine operations were anything but. He was reassured that the police had only found out about the drug business after he had ended his association with the Hull-based company, even though they could probably still link him to their earlier partnership. It also begged the question what else did the police know and how accurate was this man's intelligence?

"The good news for you Jonathon is that the official investigation has only recently begun and they are totally unaware of your other business interests, including how you recycle the gemstones through your jewellery shop and various dealers and your offshore banking arrangements. They also do not have any actual proof linking you directly to either operation, although Mr Williams will definitely be implicated because of the money trails leading back to him which they will undoubtedly uncover once the investigation is passed to the Serious Crimes Division. When they start digging into his financial records, especially when they find his suspected, though of course unproven, association with past money laundering, no doubt alarm bells will start ringing." Again he paused for a few seconds and then continued, getting down to business. "Firstly, I consider the information and warning I have provided so far merits a reward. At the very least, a resourceful man like yourself now being forewarned is in a position to avoid arrest and prosecution. Secondly, as a suggestion…"

"How much reward and how do you propose that I accomplish that?" Jonathon interrupted.

"As I was saying, secondly," continued the man smoothly, "you need to agree a realistic exit plan with your partner Mr Williams, which hopefully you have already discussed in case of such an eventuality, and you need to tie up a few loose ends. I understand the police are currently putting together an initial report before submitting it to Serious Crimes so I am confident you have a couple of weeks at least to resolve your unfortunate situation. In answer to your question about how much, one hundred thousand now and another one hundred thousand if you and Mr Williams successfully avoid prosecution, which is of course non-negotiable," he confirmed.

"You surprise me – I thought knowing my financial situation as you appear to that you would want more," the solicitor replied.

"I consider it a reasonable amount and I am not a greedy man. Like you Jonathon, I think the money is not my driving force. I do it because I enjoy it and I can."

"How do I know that the police investigation is in fact real and this is not just a very imaginative scheme to extort money from me?" Jonathon asked finally.

"A fair question which unfortunately for your peace of

mind I cannot answer without jeopardising my sources and indeed my own anonymity, so I am afraid I must ask you to take my word both in the veracity of my information and my well-intentioned motives."

Jonathon considered this but quickly realised that he did not have any option other than to accept this mysterious man's offer because if the police were not currently investigating him and he declined to pay the money, he was certain they soon would be.

"I accept your terms," the solicitor conceded. "Give me the account details and Emrys will wire the money tomorrow."

"Excellent Jonathon, I will keep you abreast of any new developments that I uncover in the investigation and look forward to a successful conclusion to your efforts to extricate yourself from this unfortunate situation."

With that, he gave Jonathon the details of a bank account in Switzerland, wished him a pleasant evening and ended the call. He then downloaded the recording he had made of their conversation onto his laptop, copied it onto a memory stick and put it into the solicitor's file, which together with Emrys's, he returned to the bottom drawer of the filing cabinet. He then removed the sim card from the phone, cut it into quarters and dropped the pieces into the waste bin by the side of his desk.

Meanwhile, on completing the call, Jonathon immediately sent a text to his partner in Swansea on their private PAYG phones: "Leave tomorrow free, need to talk. Will call you from the office at about 10.30am."

He then put the phones back in the desk drawer, stood up and left the room, closing the door behind him.

"Are you ready to go darling?" Jonathon shouted up the stairs towards their bedroom. "It's five past and I've booked the table for 8.30pm so we need to get a move on."

"On my way down," she called back and almost immediately appeared at the top of the stairs and came down to join him at the front door.

"Okay, let's go – and by the way, your new outfit is stunning and you look beautiful as always," he said and gave her a kiss on the cheek as he opened the door and ushered her outside.

Chapter 27

At 10.20am the following day, Jonathon was at his desk at the office in Manchester when he rang through to his secretary.

"Tricia, I'm going to be tied up for the next hour or so; no calls or interruptions please," he announced.

"Okay, Mr Underwood," she replied.

The solicitor took a deep breath, composed himself and then tapped in the number of his friend and partner in crime, knowing that what they were about to discuss would probably change both their lives.

"Good morning, Jonathon," came the prompt reply as the accountant answered the call after the first ring. "I presume this is not good news?" he asked anxiously.

"Good morning, Emrys. I suppose it depends on one's point of view," Jonathon replied thoughtfully. "I am certainly the bearer of some very bad news, but the fact that I am able to pass it on to you now means it could be incredibly fortunate in the long run for both of us."

Jonathon then relayed in great detail the content of the mystery man's initial text warning, their subsequent telephone conversation, the depth and range of his knowledge of their business and financial dealings, both legal and illegal, the alleged police investigation, his demands for payment and finally the predicament that they now found themselves in.

Emrys was silent for almost all of Jonathon's narrative except for the odd confirmatory question when he occasionally managed to clear his mind from the all-consuming foreboding that was slowly enveloping him and ask Jonathon to clarify some point of information.

When Jonathon finished, he sat quietly waiting for Emrys's reaction.

After what seemed like an age, Emrys spoke. "I cannot believe this – how did he find out so much about us and our dealings without us having the slightest inkling of what he was doing?" he asked in disbelief and then there was another short silence.

"Incredible," he almost whispered and then there was another silence before the accountant finally continued. "Do you believe him about the police, Jonathon?"

"Does it matter? Either way we have to pay and take the necessary actions to nullify any potential police investigation. I am certain he is telling the truth, by the way, so we have to try and plan our way out of this, and quickly. Fortunately, thanks to your foresight and planning for such an eventuality, as our anonymous informant so eloquently put it, we have our options," Jonathon replied.

"You think it's that serious, Jonathon, you think I should disappear?" his friend and business partner asked desperately.

"Yes I do unfortunately, I think it is the only way we might get away with it and live to fight another day as they say. You need to take the blame for any illegal activities they do uncover, as we discussed, and I will plead ignorance and tough it out. Our friendly informer said they have no actual evidence linking me to anything, probably lots of circumstantial stuff but nothing incriminating or solid enough to hold up in court. You disappear off to the good old US of A with the new identity you set up when you bought the two properties over there and get a nice tan hopping between Miami Beach and Grand Cayman. Then you can continue running our finances under your new identity when I engage your company after the disappearance of that criminal Emrys Williams and the dissolution of his accounting firm. Your first job when you arrive out there is to close down all the bank accounts that could be traced to our current organisation and transfer all the monies to new ones, preferably at completely different locations. Then set up some new 'shell companies' to trade through but I will leave all that to you. He assured me that we probably have at least two to three weeks grace before they start coming after us in earnest but I suggest the sooner you go the better."

"Seems like our only option," Emrys agreed. "I'll get right onto it. What are you going to do at this end?"

"According to our man, the police are only looking at Wade's and Boston's. Apparently they only have actual evidence of the package delivery from the ship to the driver at the bungalow on Anglesey. They are presuming it is then delivered to someone at Wade's by their driver from Moelfre, but they have no actual proof of it, or that it ends up at my office or who else at Wade's is involved, although they have their suspicions of course. So all I need to do is remove the driver, either permanently or to somewhere the police cannot find him. Brian Mather and John Bootle are sound and with no actual evidence against them, they should be fine. I will speak to the two of them and we will decide the best course of action for the driver," Jonathon explained.

"And the drug operation?" Emrys asked.

"I don't know about Boston's, that could be a lot trickier, especially as I am no longer involved with them fortunately. Going off the information our man has, which unknown to him is now out of date, do I tip Peter off and advise him of the investigation so he can stop the deliveries, or at least change the arrangements he now has, or do I take a chance and say nothing to him? He takes the fall with his new partners, contradicting any suspicions they might have that I am in any way involved? I'll have to give that some more thought." After a short pause the solicitor continued, "Are we agreed then Emrys?"

"Agreed," replied the accountant. "Tomorrow I will tell the office I have decided to take a couple of weeks off – that gives me plenty of time to clear everything up here and at the flat before setting up my new life over there and before anyone starts missing me. I knew being single with no attachments would be beneficial eventually," he laughed.

"Good man. Let me know when you get settled and text your new contact details to this number. Safe journey old friend and good luck," and with that, Jonathon ended the call.

It was going to be a busy day for both of them. Emrys

needed to sort out his affairs as much as possible, including transferring all the monies in his various bank accounts via several wiring operations to his new ones overseas and closing the UK ones. He gathered together all the various files, electronic equipment and phones which he would either shred or destroy before dropping them off at the local waste disposal centre before and then sat down to review the roundabout route that Colin Shaw, his new persona, would take to his new life in Miami Beach and Grand Cayman. He had decided his itinerary twelve months ago when he had made his potential escape plans but he had to check that the times of the various carriers were still current. He would go by train to London, paying cash for the ticket, and then take the Eurostar as Colin Shaw to Paris, again paying cash for his ticket, before flying to JFK New York from Charles De Gaulle Airport, arriving in the USA as Colin. Finally, he would take an internal flight down to Miami and his new life and safety.

Meanwhile, Jonathon would have to tie up as many loose ends as possible in order to distance himself, albeit temporarily, from all his illegal activities before the impending investigation. That would mainly include cancelling future deliveries from Nigeria, discussing with Brian Mather and John Bootle the best course of action concerning the disappearance of the driver Mat Dawson and the potentially more hazardous decision of how to deal with Peter Boston and the drugs – should he tell Peter or not?

He would worry about the fallout from Emrys's

disappearance, and by it his admission of guilt, when it eventually came to light. Any subsequent financial problems with his business dealings would be dealt with as they arose but that shouldn't prove too difficult as by that time Emrys should have established the new bank accounts and trading companies in Grand Cayman from his base in Miami Beach. Everything else relating to the jewellery shop in Manchester, the gallery in London, the auction house in the Midlands and his other businesses around the country would continue trading legally until the investigation into his affairs was terminated due to a lack of any concrete evidence.

Yes, with a bit of luck and a fair wind, he and Emrys would be okay. His only lingering concern was his mysterious caller. Emrys had wired the initial payment of £100,000 as instructed which on arrival in Switzerland had almost immediately been transferred twice more before finally settling in a numbered account in the Isle of Man. Jonathon had received a text from a new number confirming the money's arrival, thanking him for his prompt payment and ending with a promise to keep in touch. Whether he could trust the man and if he would prove a problem in the future were questions that were of great concern to Jonathon moving forward but as there was nothing he could do to resolve that situation at the moment he put them aside for the time being.

Chapter 28

Chief Superintendent Jonny Radcliffe arrived for his appointment with the Chief Constable promptly at 2pm carrying a large manila folder containing eight neatly typed documents, two copies of each of the four separate reports. He knocked on the door and entered the large, richly furnished office as the Chief Constable rose from his chair behind his antique oak desk and moved towards him.

"Afternoon, Jonny," he greeted his number two, holding out his hand.

"Afternoon, Sir," Jonny replied as they shook hands and then sat down on either side of the desk.

"What have you got for me?" the Chief Constable asked.

The Chief Superintendent took the eight reports out of the folder and handed four of them to his superior, labelled Boston Heating & Ventilating Supplies, Wade Manufacturing Limited, Retired DCI J W Thomas and CS J Radcliffe.

"DCI Thomas's report is the one our retired detective who initiated the investigation kindly supplied and outlines everything he and his friend Steve Guest uncovered and passed on to you and William Wade at your meeting in Moelfre. This includes Underwood's and Williams's backgrounds, various business relationships and the alleged gemstone smuggling and drugs operations. The Wade

Manufacturing report contains photographic confirmation of the delivery of a package from the *MV Caracas* to the bungalow on Anglesey but only circumstantial evidence that the package is then delivered to Wade's. In my report, as you can see, with the help of William at the Wade's depot we observed what we believe is the probable passage of the package firstly from the driver to John Bootle the Transport Manager at Wade's, then to Brian Mather the Operations Director and then onto Jonathon Underwood in Manchester. Unfortunately, apart from the during the initial delivery to the bungalow at Moelfre from the ship, no one actually saw the cylinder again and when Underwood finally left his office after his meeting with the Operations Director, which is when we presume Mather passed the gemstones to him, he was not carrying anything as my photograph clearly shows. That surprised me as I wouldn't have thought, if he indeed had been passed the precious stones, that he would have left such a valuable package overnight in his office."

"Yes I agree, Jonny, but perhaps he has somewhere very secure in his office, a safe or some other kind of fortified strongbox, where he stores them before passing them on at a later date to a third party, probably somewhere in Manchester. Pity about no actual sighting of the package at Wade's or Underwood's but I think we can be sure that is how it is delivered."

"Yes Sir, I agree. Moving on to Boston's. Again, we have lots of new photographic evidence showing where we think the drugs are initially picked up in Amsterdam and them being delivered to Boston's and then distributed to the depots in London and the Midlands. Once we are in position to enter and search these various locations, I am convinced we will find all the evidence we need. One thing to note from that report though – you will see that there is no mention of McConnell Transport & Warehousing Limited, Underwood's company from Liverpool which appeared to handle the drug deliveries from Boston's when our friends from Anglesey originally uncovered the operation, which further tied Underwood to the drug dealing operation. The vans which took the suspect crates had no markings and, as I said, went to destinations in Potters Bar and Sutton Coldfield not Liverpool."

"Yes, I see what you are saying, Jonny – there is a lot of new circumstantial evidence confirming our various suspicions of what is going on but nothing concrete which ties Underwood directly to anything other than being these companies' solicitor," the Chief Constable reasoned.

"Exactly, Sir. Like you, I am convinced he and the Swansea accountant are at the heart of this and no doubt other criminal operations which as yet we don't know about. In my opinion, we definitely have enough to pass it over to Serious Crimes," the Chief Superintendent concluded. "Once they begin a full surveillance operation, including bank, internet, email and phone call checks, I am sure they will turn up all the evidence they need for criminal convictions for the gemstone smuggling, drugs distribution and who knows what else," the Chief Superintendent concluded.

There was a period of silence while the Chief Constable

read through the four reports before finally speaking again.

"I agree Jonny, leave it with me. Great work in putting this all together in such a short time." He stood up and showed his number two to the door. "I'll keep you informed," he said. After shaking hands, Chief Superintendent Radcliffe left the office. The Chief Constable returned to his desk, picked up his phone and called New Scotland Yard in London to set up a meeting with the Serious Crimes Division.

Chapter 29

After ending the call with his partner in Swansea, Jonathon sat back and considered his options.

His first priority was the Wade's driver and what to do with him as he was one of the few potentially weak links in the organisation. He picked up his work phone and called Brian Mather on his mobile.

"Morning, Brian," Jonathon spoke cheerily when the Wade's Operations Director answered the call. "I trust you are well?" he asked.

"Yes thank you, Jonathon, and to what do I owe this unexpected pleasure?" he answered.

"Now, now Brian, sarcasm does not become you old chap," Jonathon replied, "but since you ask, would it be possible for you to pop over to my office for a quick chat as soon as?"

Brian was immediately alert. "I was just on my way out to a meeting, Jonathon – can it wait?"

"Not really, old chap," Jonathon said. "Could you possibly rearrange your meeting for another day? I really would appreciate it if you could pop over now," Jonathon insisted.

Brian was now concerned and quickly replied, "No problem, Jonathon, I'll make a quick phone call and be right over."

"Excellent, Brian, see you shortly," and the solicitor ended the call.

His next call was to Peter Boston. Jonathon had decided to inform Peter of the police interest in the drugs operation and give him time to either make alternative import and distribution arrangements or postpone them entirely for the time being. Jonathon had decided that Peter's new partners were not the sort of people to upset or cause any major problems to and resolved that by giving Peter the tip-off, he reduced the possibility of any fall-out coming his way from any subsequent investigation because of his recent involvement with the Hull-based company.

After the initial shock, Peter thanked Jonathon profusely for the tip-off and promised to shut down the operation completely. He agreed with Jonathon that his new partners would not be happy with any sort of police investigation and it also left open the door for any possible future dealings with them.

Jonathon then took one of the PAYG phones from his desk and sent a short text to the only number in the contact directory: "Please suspend all my deliveries until further notice. Recommend perhaps you find alternative carrier. Caracas under surveillance."

Thirty minutes after sending the text, his office manager rang through on the internal phone line. "Mr Underwood, Mr Mather is here for you."

"Thank you Tricia, ask him to come through please," the solicitor replied.

As Brian entered his office, Jonathon stood up and stepped forward to meet him. "Thank you for coming so promptly Brian," he said as he shook Brian's hand and then closed the door behind him. "Please take a seat."

Jonathon went back behind his desk and sat down again.

"Unfortunately I have some bad news. It would appear that the police have become interested in our little operation out at Anglesey," Jonathon started.

"What!" exclaimed Brian. "How?"

"Quietly please, Brian, no need to get upset, everything is under control," Jonathon reassured him, although inwardly he was not yet certain that he would come out of this completely unscathed. "I will fill you in with all the necessary details in due course, suffice to say that I am confident that we can sort everything out satisfactorily. Our immediate problem is your driver, Mat Dawson. I understand he is the only person that the police have any hard evidence against at the moment. We need to make him disappear as quickly as possible. We still have some time to organise things so the decision we have to make today is what do we do with him?" Jonathon paused and waited for Brian to speak.

"What do you mean by 'disappear', Jonathon?" Brian asked cautiously.

"I mean if we move him to a new location, perhaps with a new identity, can he be trusted to keep our illicit operations to himself or do we need a more permanent solution?" the solicitor replied.

"Mat is a good lad Jonathon and I am sure he could be

trusted to keep his mouth shut," Brian replied, not wanting to consider the more permanent option that Jonathon was appearing to suggest.

"You would stake your future on that would you Brian? Because that is what you would be doing, not to mention mine."

"Yes," Brian confirmed. He liked Mat and did not want to think what might happen to him if Jonathon decided to remove him completely.

"Right Brian," Jonathon decided, "in that case, you need to get John Bootle to go down to Anglesey and pick Mat up and take him to some short-term accommodation which I will arrange while we find somewhere more permanent for him to stay. I will sort out a new identity for him later if we deem it necessary. We need to make sure the cottage is completely cleaned of anything remotely linked to Mat or Wade's. Then you will have to organise a new driver to take over Mat's duties."

"No problem, Harry Grimes can take over the deliveries for now. He did the Dublin run in the early days and he can be trusted to keep his mouth shut if the police start asking any questions. How do we explain Mat's sudden disappearance?"

"Get him to write a letter of resignation saying he has decided to do some travelling or something like that. Then you can say it came out of the blue, he handed in his resignation and just left that day. He's self-employed isn't he, so there would be no question of a notice period being required, just the inconvenience of you finding someone to take over his duties."

"That would work," agreed Brian.

"Right, that's about everything for today Brian. I must emphasise that it is imperative that Mat disappears as soon as possible, this weekend would be ideal. I will let you know where to take him later on today," Jonathon concluded and showed Brian to the door. "Just carry on as normal and I will keep you informed of any other developments. Speak to you later," and with that, Brian left and Jonathon closed the door behind him.

Jonathon had toyed with the idea of telling Brian about Emrys's imminent disappearance and subsequent shouldering of the blame for any charges which might arise from the police investigation but he had decided against it for the moment. He would divulge that part of the plan later when he deemed it necessary.

The solicitor went over the plan he and Emrys had formulated again in his head and concluded they had done everything possible to cover their tracks. He would now just have to sit tight and wait for the inevitable events to unfold.

Chapter 30

Jonathon received the text he had been waiting for on the new PAYG phone seven days later: "Arrived safely. Accounts and companies closed. New ones will be opened and active shortly. New contact details to follow. Awaiting further instructions. Hope all good at your end. CS"

Mat Dawson was now living in accommodation just outside Poole in Dorset, rented under the name of one of Underwood's other companies based nearby. He had been taken on as a temporary driver under an assumed name until Jonathon decided on a more permanent solution to Mat's relocation. The solicitor had also briefed Brian Mather on the plan to let Emrys take all the blame for anything that the police might uncover regarding the gemstone and drug smuggling, leaving them reasonably in the clear, albeit under suspicion, but with nothing that could be proven in court. He had given the Operations Director few actual details of Emrys's disappearance or their future plans, just enough to keep him happy and secure in the knowledge that he himself would be safe from any possible prosecution.

With everything now in place, Jonathon was ready to embark on the next stage of their plan. It was just over two weeks since Emrys had informed his office that he had decided to take a two-week break and do a tour of the highlands of Scotland, something he had told them he had always wanted to do. It also gave a plausible reason why his office had not been able to contact him by phone or email during the two weeks, due to the poor or non-existent mobile and internet coverage in that remote area of the UK, but they were now becoming concerned about his continuing absence and lack of communication with them.

Jonathon called through to his secretary. "Tricia, please could you get me Brian Mather at Wade's."

"Certainly, Mr Underwood."

A couple of minutes later his internal phone line rang. "I have Mr Mather for you."

"Thank you, Tricia," Jonathon replied. "Hello Brian, are you well?" he asked the Operations Director at Wade Manufacturing.

"Yes thanks Jonathon, what can I do for you?"

"You need to call an emergency meeting of the board – it would appear that Emrys Williams has gone missing," Jonathon announced. They had already discussed how they would play this so Brian knew what he was supposed to do.

"Right, Jonathon, I will speak to William and Jo right away and see if we can organise something for tomorrow here at Wade's."

"Excellent, Brian, speak to you soon," and with that, they ended the call.

Twenty minutes later, Brian rang back on the main office number to inform Jonathon that the meeting was arranged for ten o'clock the following morning. As agreed between them, Brian had not given any details regarding the meeting to William and Joanne, just that Jonathon had called it and stressed the urgency.

At 9.55am the next day, Jonathon was shown into the boardroom at Wade Manufacturing Limited to be met by three very serious looking company directors, although one of them was already privy to what was about to unfold. Brian immediately stood up, went over to Jonathon and shook his hand. "Good morning Jonathon, I presume you have a very good reason for this?" asked the Operations Director.

Jonathon smiled to himself, impressed with Brian's apparent outward appearance of concern. "Yes indeed Brian and thank you to everyone for responding so promptly to my request."

"Would you like a drink, Jonathon? Perhaps I should order tea for everyone?" asked Joanna.

"Yes, that would be great, Joanna, an excellent idea," replied the company solicitor.

Joanna went to the door and called over to Sue Greenhalgh, Brian's PA, and asked her to organise some tea and biscuits.

"What is this all about?" William asked brusquely, looking at Jonathon.

"Let's just wait for the tea, Dad," Joanna said, "then we can all relax and find out what is on Jonathon's mind."

They all stood around in an uncomfortable silence until shortly afterwards Sue appeared with a tray containing a pot of tea, four cups and saucers, spoons, a small milk jug, sugar bowl and a large plate of biscuits. When Sue had left and Joanna had poured the tea, the three directors and the solicitor took their places around the boardroom table: William at the head, Joanna and Brian on one side and Jonathon directly across from them.

Jonathon paused for a moment to let the tension build a little then opened the meeting.

"I will get straight to the point," he began. "I think we have a problem. I called our accountant's office in Swansea yesterday regarding a query I had about the new warehouse building we are acquiring for Joanna's new online catalogue business and it would appear that Emrys has gone missing. Apparently he went on holiday just over two weeks ago, touring around Scotland I believe, and they have not heard from him since he left the office that Friday. He should have been back three days ago but, as I said, they have not heard a thing from him – no call, text or email, nothing."

"Do you think he might have had an accident Jonathon?" Brian asked on cue.

"No idea Brian, but it is very strange. As he's a single man, he probably hasn't been missed apart from by his office. They had no idea of his proposed holiday plans so of course there is no one to call to see where he might be or has been. As a precaution, I suggested to his secretary that she should call their local police, which she later confirmed that she had done."

"How does this affect us, Jonathon?" Brian asked, again on cue.

210

"It doesn't immediately as I understand it," the solicitor replied. "The sale on the warehouse has gone through and all payments have been made. Obviously Emrys handles all your financial affairs but in the short term, having spoken to his office, there is nothing outstanding and he has a junior partner who can handle any queries that may arise until his return."

"Is that it?" asked William.

"Yes, for the moment," replied Jonathon. "I hope you don't think I was a little dramatic requesting the meeting but I thought it of sufficient importance to meet up face to face and then I could answer any questions that you may have."

"Like you said, nothing to panic about," said William. "Probably just decided to have a few extra days away." With that, he stood up, left the room and returned to his office where he immediately closed the door, took out his mobile and called Chief Constable Bright. The call went to his voicemail service and William left a message for his new friend to ring him urgently.

William's phone rang almost immediately; it was the Chief Constable.

"Thanks for calling back, Leo," William said on answering the call. "I have just come out of a meeting with Jonathon Underwood, Brian and Joanna. Underwood has just informed us that the accountant Emrys Williams appears to have gone missing and Underwood has advised the accountant's office to inform the local police down in Swansea. I thought you should know."

"Thanks for that, Bill, very interesting. I will pass it on. Let me know if you hear anything else," replied the Chief Constable who ended the call and immediately asked his secretary to call his contact at New Scotland Yard to inform him of this new development.

When this news was passed to the leader of the task force assigned to the investigation into the potential illegal operations of Jonathon Underwood, he immediately arranged a meeting with the team leaders and his superior as the warning flags had already started appearing regarding the investigation. The disappearance of one of the suspected main players confirmed that something was definitely amiss.

To date, the surveillance team covering Boston Heating & Ventilation Supplies had not seen any vans going over to Rotterdam on the ferry or white Transits travelling down to Potters Bar or Sutton Coldfield, and the *MV Caracas* had anchored in the bay off Moelfre the previous Monday and Tuesday and there had been no nocturnal comings and goings from the ship before it set off again on its way to Liverpool. Plus, there had been no activity at the bungalow in Moelfre since the surveillance team had arrived a week earlier and they had also learnt that the driver, Mat Dawson, who had been photographed receiving the package from the *Caracas*, had handed his notice in a couple of weeks ago and then completely disappeared. Finally, one of the team in the guise of a hiker had walked past the cottage and after having a quick look through all the windows thought that it looked unoccupied.

The meeting, once convened, did not last long. After a

brief discussion, they were all in agreement that it now appeared with this latest news that it was Emrys Williams who must be at the heart of any illegal activity not Jonathon Underwood. They concluded that he must somehow have learnt about their investigation and closed the gemstone smuggling and drug importation operations down before, together with Mat Dawson, disappearing to goodness knows where – and, since they had a couple of weeks head start, they could be anywhere in the world right now. They decided it was pointless to continue the surveillance on the ship and the Moelfre cottage and also stood the Hull team down. They agreed they would pass the relevant information and reports regarding the drug importation and gemstone smuggling to the Hull and Manchester forces so that they could continue with any local investigations into Wade's and Boston's if they deemed it appropriate. They would also liaise with the Swansea police on the accountant's disappearance and continue with their investigation into his financial dealings in case they could find anything worth pursuing. With that, they ended the meeting and closed their investigation.

The following day, Chief Constable Bright received a call from his colleague at New Scotland Yard informing him of all the new developments and the decision to stand the teams down and close the investigation into Jonathon Underwood. He explained that they were continuing to look into Emrys Williams's affairs and he would continue to be the subject of an international search and arrest warrant. The Chief Constable thanked him for letting him know and immediately put a call through to Chief Superintendent Radcliffe.

"Morning, Jonny," the Chief Constable greeted his number two.

"Morning, Sir. What can I do for you?" he replied.

"Just calling to let you know that the main investigation into Underwood and Williams has been dropped. I've just had a call from my man at Scotland Yard and they now believe that it was Williams who was running the show and not Underwood. They believe that the accountant must have got wind of the investigation, closed everything down and disappeared off into the sunset before we could get to him."

"That's a surprise, Sir, I was sure it was Underwood," replied a smiling Radcliffe. "Disappointing we let him slip – was there nothing we could get anyone on?"

"Apparently not. The driver who was photographed receiving the package from the ship at Moelfre also did a runner so we were left with nothing that could incriminate anyone at Wade's or Boston's. The file is still open on Williams and there is an international warrant out both on him and the van driver but they have both disappeared completely. They will of course question Underwood, Brian Mather, John Bootle and Peter Boston, but without actual evidence they have no case to take to court. They have their suspicions of course, the same as ours, but no proof."

"Thanks for letting me know Sir, just have to put it down as one that got away," the Chief Superintendent replied and with that they ended the call.

The Chief Constable then called the retired Detective

Chief Inspector on his mobile.

John Wyn Thomas answered the call on the fourth ring. "Good morning Chief Constable," John said, seeing his name on his phone's screen.

"Good morning, John, can you speak?" the Cheshire policeman replied.

"Yes, go ahead."

"Just rang to let you know that unfortunately we have had to drop the investigation into Jonathon Underwood and his various business operations. Without divulging too much confidential information, there is no case to answer. Williams and the Wade's driver have both disappeared and are still being investigated but there is no firm evidence linking Underwood or anyone at Wade's or Boston's to anything illegal, just a lot of very strong suspicions. But as you know, we can't arrest and convict anyone on suspicions."

"They obviously got wind of the investigation then," John quickly concluded. "Any news on DS Watkins and his ties to Underwood?"

"It would appear so," said the Chief Constable. "Strangely enough, he put his papers in a few weeks ago, taking early retirement I believe. Again, there is no hard evidence against him and, as we are not charging Underwood, he is in the clear with a full pension, plus anything he might get from the solicitor for his silence of course. At least that's one less bad apple in the force. Thanks again for all your input John and if anything new does come to light, I will be sure to let you know." And with that, he ended the call.

John Wyn Thomas immediately called his partner in crime Steve Guest and updated him on the latest developments which they both agreed were a great disappointment after all their hard work uncovering the apparent, and to them obvious, illegal activities. They sadly conceded there was nothing more they could do about it and agreed to meet up that evening at their favourite watering hole as usual to discuss the whole affair and their part in it.

Chapter 31

Three weeks after Chief Constable Bright informed Chief Superintendent Radcliffe that the investigation into Jonathon Underwood had been closed, and with no further action having been taken against him, Jonathon was sitting at his office desk in Manchester when his private mobile rang showing 'Caller Withheld'. After a slight pause, he answered after the fourth ring and immediately recognised the smooth tones of his mysterious informant.

"Good evening Jonathon, well I trust?" the voice asked.

"Yes thank you and you?" he replied.

"I am fine thank you. Still at work Jonathon, you are a conscientious solicitor," the voice continued. "Just thought I would call for a quick catch up. I believe you owe me the outstanding balance of £100,000. I have been reliably informed that the investigation into your business operations has been closed although there is an outstanding warrant for your colleague Emrys Williams which, as we both know, will be hard to serve as our dear Emrys is no more, figuratively speaking," the man laughed. "By the way, how is Colin?"

"You are incredibly well informed," Jonathon admitted, shocked that he already knew Emrys's new identity.

"It is my business to know, Jonathon," the confident voice continued. "Intelligence is the most important weapon in war or business don't you think?"

"Do you want the money wiring to the same bank account?" the solicitor asked, eager to keep the call as short as possible.

"No, I will text you the new account details immediately after our call concludes."

"In that case, I will say goodbye. Hopefully I will not require your services again," Jonathon said and ended the call.

Almost immediately, an incoming text message appeared on his phone giving him the new bank account details which he then forwarded to Emrys for the payment of the outstanding £100,000, hoping it would be the last time he had any dealings with his mysterious informant.

As Jonathon was texting the bank details, the informant was updating the accountant's file, which he had just retrieved from the bottom drawer of the filing cabinet, with Emrys Williams's new name, addresses in Miami Beach and Grand Cayman, his main phone and email contact details, and details of the newly formed 'shell companies' and their respective offshore bank accounts from the email he had recently received. On completing the new information, he closed the file again and sat looking out of his study window over the lush Cheshire countryside as he thoughtfully tapped his right index finger on the file cover, smiling to himself.

ABOUT THE AUTHOR

I am married to Jan, my wife of 34 years, and have two sons, Andrew 31 and Mathew 30.

I was born in Hyde, Tameside (formerly Cheshire), 69 years ago and went to St George's infants and primary school and then on to Hyde County Grammar School. I spent the majority of my working life as a Sales and Marketing professional and fully retired three years ago and moved down to live on Anglesey one year later with Jan from our home in Lancashire.

Printed in Great Britain
by Amazon

16883493R00131